Praise for Stephanie Bond

"The perfect summer read."
—*Romance Reviews Today* on
Sand, Sun...Seduction!

"Sex and humor blend perfectly...this fairy tale
of a story has the perfect magic ending."
—*RT Book Reviews* on *No Peeking...*

"Blazing hot...will have you planning
your own fantasy."
—*Cataromance* on *In a Bind*

"A burning-hot hero, and the sex explodes."
—*RT Book Reviews* on *Watch and Learn*

"The next fantasy will be anticipated
with bated breath!"
—*Cataromance* on *Watch and Learn*

Dear Reader,

Have you given up on love? Carol Snow has, burned
by a marriage proposal that went up in flames on
Valentine's Day. Since that time, she's worked for a
greeting card company, helping to bring words of
hope to others, while keeping her own heart tucked
away. When the members of her erotic book club
are challenged to seduce the men of their dreams,
she bends to peer pressure by faking a seduction
of hunky coworker Luke Chancellor—who's going
to know that she doesn't plan to go through with it?
Then a magical blizzard, a bump on the head and
a visit to Valentine's Days past, present and future
change everything....

I hope you enjoy this story that's part fantasy,
part reality and wholly romantic! Please tell your
friends about the great love stories you find
between the pages of Harlequin romance novels.
Thanks very much for your support—visit me at
www.stephaniebond.com.

With love and laughter,

Stephanie Bond

Stephanie Bond

HER SEXY VALENTINE

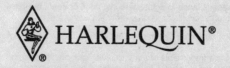

HARLEQUIN®

TORONTO • NEW YORK • LONDON
AMSTERDAM • PARIS • SYDNEY • HAMBURG
STOCKHOLM • ATHENS • TOKYO • MILAN • MADRID
PRAGUE • WARSAW • BUDAPEST • AUCKLAND

Recycling programs
for this product may
not exist in your area.

ISBN-13: 978-0-373-79526-0

HER SEXY VALENTINE

Copyright © 2010 by Stephanie Bond, Inc.

ABOUT THE AUTHOR

Stephanie Bond lives in a modern loft in midtown Atlanta but still believes in old-fashioned true love and happy endings.

Books by Stephanie Bond

HARLEQUIN BLAZE
   2—TWO SEXY!
169—MY FAVORITE MISTAKE
282—JUST DARE ME...
338—SHE DID A BAD, BAD THING
428—WATCH AND LEARN
434—IN A BIND
440—NO PEEKING...
500—SEDUCTION BY THE BOOK

MIRA BOOKS
BODY MOVERS
BODY MOVERS: 2 BODIES FOR THE PRICE OF 1
BODY MOVERS: 3 MEN AND A BODY
4 BODIES AND A FUNERAL
5 BODIES TO DIE FOR
6 KILLER BODIES

Don't miss any of our special offers. Write to us at the following address for information on our newest releases.

Harlequin Reader Service
U.S.: 3010 Walden Ave., P.O. Box 1325, Buffalo, NY 14269
Canadian: P.O. Box 609, Fort Erie, Ont. L2A 5X3

For Blake, whose creative heart will be missed...

1

This Valentine's Day, Cupid will take no prisoners...

Carol Snow picked up the cartoonish card sitting on her assistant's desk that featured the celebrated cherub wearing fatigues, with bow and arrow at the ready. She idly opened the card to glance at the message inside.

So your best strategy is to surrender. A white flag waved feebly in the background. The name "Stan" was scrawled across the bottom.

Carol frowned and turned over the valentine, not wholly surprised to discover it was a product of the company she worked for, Mystic Touch Greeting Cards. Stan must also be an employee. She set the card back on the cluttered desk, rankled by the cheerful sentimentality. Thank goodness she didn't have to work on the creative side of the business and be surrounded by that inane fluff all day.

Carol leveled an irritated glance in the direction of her assistant Tracy who had her back turned, whispering low into the phone, where, as far as Carol could tell, was how the young woman had spent most of her day. Carol rolled her eyes—a new boyfriend, no doubt. Probably Stan, the guy who'd sent the valentine. Tamping down her growing frustration, Carol glanced at her watch—at this rate, she'd be late for the monthly meeting of the Red Tote Book Club.

She cleared her throat meaningfully. Tracy cupped her hand over the mouthpiece of the phone and turned in her chair, her face lined with trepidation. "Yes, Ms. Snow?"

"I need to talk to you about this project before I leave."

"Okay."

Carol pursed her mouth at the woman's pause. "And I need to leave now."

Tracy glanced at the clock. "But it's only six…you usually stay until eight or nine."

Carol stiffened at the woman's tone that smacked of an indictment on her personal life. "Not tonight."

"Are you sick?"

Carol frowned. "No. Would you please hang up so we can talk?"

Tracy uncovered the mouthpiece and murmured something low before returning the handset to the receiver. "What's up?"

Carol bit down on the inside of her cheek. "*What's up* is this memo for the quarterly report. It's riddled with typos." She handed over the piece of paper where she'd circled the errors with a red marker.

Tracy bit her lip. "Oh. I'll redo it."

"I want a clean version on my desk when I arrive tomorrow morning," Carol chided.

"Yes, ma'am."

"And Tracy? You've been spending a lot of time on the phone—that puts both of us behind."

The young woman nodded. "Yes, ma'am. I'm sorry."

Carol made a rueful noise, then retreated into her office. Appointed with dark furniture, it was spacious and fitting for the director of Finance. A box window provided a nice view of the Atlanta skyline while leaving enough wall space for the banks of extra wide file cabinets that lined the room.

She straightened her already tidy desk, then retrieved her purse, briefcase and the red tote of books for her book club meeting. When she strode past Tracy's desk, Carol gasped in dismay to see the woman was on the phone again. Shaking her head, Carol walked up to the elevator and stabbed the button. Tracy was going to be sorely disappointed if she continued to put her love life before her job.

Men. Could. Not. Be. Trusted.

Somebody in the creative department ought to put *that* sentiment on a Mystic Touch card.

The elevator dinged and the doors opened, revealing a sole occupant: Luke Chancellor, Director of Sales and resident playboy. A grin spread over his handsome face. "Going home early, Snow? You must have a hot date for a cold Tuesday night."

Carol stuck her tongue in her cheek—she was not in the mood to be teased. "Actually, Chancellor, I've decided to take the stairs."

She turned and stalked to the stairwell, ignoring the man's booming laughter. Luke Chancellor was an outrageous flirt who seemed to have made her his pet project. In an effort to avoid him, Carol jogged down the stairs as fast as her high heels would allow. When she reached the lobby, she was relieved to see the elevator hadn't yet arrived. Juggling the items in her arms, she scooted out the front door of the office building and in the direction of her car. If every traffic light between Buckhead and downtown Atlanta was green, she *might* make it to the book club meeting on time.

"Hey, Carol!"

At the sound of Luke's voice behind her, Carol winced and kept moving. But in her haste, her red stiletto heel caught a raised edge on the sidewalk and she stumbled. Her brief-case, book tote and purse went flying, and she flailed, mentally bracing herself to hit the pavement hard. At the last possible second, though, a pair of strong arms kept her from falling flat on her face.

"I got you," Luke whispered in her ear like a warm breeze in the February chill.

The scent of his earthy cologne curled into her lungs, compromising her breathing. Her body distantly registered the fact that his big hands were touching her, his fingers burning into the skin of her shoulders and brushing her breasts through the layers of her prim suit. Unbidden lust shot through her midsection, reminding Carol how long it had been since she'd been so close to a man. The alien sensation jolted her into action.

"Let go of me," she said through gritted teeth, pulling free of his grasp. She straightened and patted at her clothing.

Luke's legendary mouth quirked into a half-smile. "You're welcome," he said drily, then crouched to gather her things from the ground.

He wore a mocha-colored suit that set off his dark hair and brown eyes. A handful of red silk tie poked out of his pocket, a stab at the formal corporate culture of the company. The man was known for his casual management style and practical jokes. Luke had come to Mystic Touch Greeting Cards two years ago and had leapfrogged through the ranks until he was now a peer of Carol's, a fellow director. The feminist in her had wanted to cry foul on a couple of his promotions, but admittedly, since his arrival, Luke had been instrumental in turning around the flagging sales force.

With only a few days to go until their biggest card-selling day of the year—Valentine's Day—the company was enjoying record-breaking profits. As a numbers woman, she grudgingly respected his accomplishments.

Feeling contrite, Carol stooped to help him with her things. "Sorry," she murmured. "You startled me. Thank you for…catching me."

"No problem," he said easily. "I probably distracted you when I yelled."

"Yes," she agreed, scooping up her purse and briefcase. "What did you want, Luke? I'm late for my book club."

"Whoa." He held up the books that had fallen out of her tote bag and lay scattered on the sidewalk. *Lady Chatterley's Lover? Venus in Furs? Fanny Hill? The Slave?"* A devilish grin split his face. "What kind of book club do you belong to?"

Heat climbed her face. "None of your business."

He leaned in close. "Do you accept male members?" His tone was innocent, but his eyes danced with mirth at the double entendre.

Instead of responding, Carol tried to snatch the classic erotic volumes, but he held them out of reach. Indignant anger whipped through her. "What are you, ten years old? Give me my books!"

He wagged his eyebrows as he perused the risqué covers. "I knew there was a wild side to you, Snow. You just keep it all bottled up."

Exasperated, Carol realized the best way to diffuse him was to deflect his attention. She crossed her arms. "What did you want, Chancellor?"

As if to answer her question, his dark gaze flitted over her appreciably, stirring up little flutters of awareness in its wake. With great resolve, she managed to maintain a cool expression of disdain.

Luke sighed and his shoulders sagged in defeat. "Okay, back to business. I thought it might be nice to have a company party for Valentine's Day."

She squinted. "Valentine's Day?"

"Why not? We could have it Friday."

"Friday the thirteenth?"

He shrugged. "Close enough. Valentine's is a significant sales day on our calendar. Plus a party would be a good occasion to pass out bonuses—what do you think?"

"I think this company has never issued bonuses," she chirped.

"Not in the past," he agreed. "But Mystic has had such a good year, I thought it'd be fair to spread the love, if you know what I mean. I'm sure the rest of the directors would agree with me."

Ire shot through Carol—doling out bonuses from money that Luke was being given credit for bringing in almost single-handedly would make him a bona fide hero in the eyes of the five hundred or so employees. The man would be Chief Executive Officer before the end of the year…dammit.

Squaring her shoulders, she drew upon her most authoritative voice. "In my opinion, the more prudent move for the long-term health of the company is to take the profits we make on good years and reinvest them in new technology."

His seemingly permanent grin never wavered. "In *my* opinion, you should skip your naughty book club and we should discuss this over drinks."

The pull of his body on hers was unmistakable. His decadent brown eyes were almost hypnotic, summoning her to follow him anywhere. Her breasts pinged in response and her thighs quickened. Her mouth opened and to her horror, she realized she was on the verge of saying yes.

Carol's head snapped back. "That's not going to happen." The words came out more forcefully than she'd planned—for her own benefit? "We can discuss the party and the bonuses at the directors' meeting in the morning—with an audience."

He frowned. "You're no fun."

She extended her hand, palm up, and wiggled her fingers. "My books, please?"

He relinquished his hold as if they were favorite toys. "I've never been second place to a book before."

"That you know of." Carol gave him a tight smile as she slipped the erotic books inside the red tote bag. "Goodbye, Chancellor." She turned and walked toward her car, certain now that she'd be late for the book club meeting because of the bothersome man.

"Instead of reading about life, you should try the real thing sometime!" Luke called behind her.

Carol was tempted to turn and shoot him the bird, but, mindful of their location and the curious stares they'd already garnered from employees loitering in the parking lot, she kept walking. She didn't want to keep the members of the Red Tote Book Club waiting.

And she didn't want to give Luke Chancellor the satisfaction of seeing the sudden tears his parting comment had brought to her eyes.

2

Every traffic light between Carol's office and downtown Atlanta was, not surprisingly, red. If it was the city's idea of commemorating Valentine's Day, Carol thought wryly, it was fitting that she was caught in the bottleneck. As expected, she arrived late for the meeting of the Red Tote Book Club.

So late, in fact, that she sat in the parking lot of the branch of the Atlanta Public Library where the group met and contemplated driving away. She glanced over at the box of almond cookies sitting in the passenger seat that she'd brought for the members to share and rationalized the goodies would make her a fair dinner—almonds were chock-full of fiber...

weren't they? Considering what was waiting for her inside, she was suddenly gripped with the compulsion to drop out of the group altogether. The other women wouldn't miss her. They might even be glad if she left.

They were probably sitting in there now, talking about her, the rogue member who refused to go along with the experiment their coordinator had suggested: That each member apply the lessons they'd learned from the pages of the erotic novels they'd read to seduce the man of their dreams.

The other women had embraced the challenge wholeheartedly. She, on the other hand... not so much.

Her phone chimed and she looked down to see a text message had arrived.

Are you stuck in traffic? We didn't want to start without you. Gabrielle.

Gabrielle was the coordinator of the Red Tote Book Club. Carol couldn't stop the relieved smile that curved her mouth—they did care. She quickly texted back that she'd be there in a few minutes, then grabbed the box of cookies and the red tote holding the precious books that had filled her lonely evenings over the past few months. After exiting her car, she jogged toward the entrance of the library.

Inside, she stopped to inhale the pungent scent of books and absorb the pleasant hum of computers and lowered voices. She'd been an avid reader most of her young life, but had gotten away from pleasure reading as an adult. When she'd seen the ad for the book club for women looking to add a little spice to their reading life, she'd been intrigued, if a little suspicious. But the group of women who'd gathered on that first night were amazingly like her—in their thirties, educated and single.

Except, *un*like her, they all seemed to be in the market for a boyfriend or a lover, neither of which appealed to her.

Carol wound her way through a maze of hallways to reach the tucked away room where the group met for ultimate privacy. Their book selections and discussions weren't meant for tender eyes and ears. She rapped on the door and a few seconds later, it opened wide enough to reveal the wary, blue-eyed gaze of Cassie Goodwin, fellow member. Cassie's wariness immediately turned into a smile as she opened the door and welcomed Carol inside where the other three club members—Page Sharpe, Wendy Trainer and Jacqueline Mays—sat around a table, with the group's coordinator, Gabrielle Pope, at the head.

"We were just having a toast for Gabrielle," Cassie sang, handing Carol a glass of red wine—contraband smuggled in for the occasion.

Taking a seat at the table, Carol glanced at Gabrielle and noticed the woman had a glow about her. Which could only mean one thing: Even their plain, bun-packing, cardigan-wearing leader had bagged a man. Dread settled in Carol's stomach.

"The toast isn't for me," Gabrielle fussed, although she was clearly pleased by the attention. "To seduction by the book!"

Carol was the last to lift her glass and her smile felt stiff as she looked around the table. Over the past few months, the other four members had chosen erotic books to help guide them in their sensual journey to seduce a man. Now, even their leader Gabrielle had found her match in a lover and, if the light in the woman's eyes was any indication, had found love as well.

And the cheese stands alone, Carol mused wryly as she drank deeply from the glass of merlot. She remained the lone holdout, refusing to go along with the optional assignment.

The women chorused good wishes and congratulations to Gabrielle and listened as their coordinator relayed happy details about her lover and how their relationship had taken off once they discovered common sexual ground. The woman spoke openly about tantric experiences, mirroring the frank, honest discussions the members had shared about the group's book selections. Gabrielle had declared no topic and no language was off-limits. And while Carol conceded that the candid dialogue had riveted her, she acknowledged that she'd participated less than anyone. And she'd sensed the other women were resentful to varying degrees that she'd observed more than she'd partaken.

As Gabrielle shared the lush aspects of her new relationship, Carol felt excluded. The other women leaned into each other and seemed to share an emotional shorthand she wasn't privy to. It occurred to her that they didn't trust her because she'd refused to be vulnerable, refused to take the same risk they'd taken.

Carol shrank back in her chair, suddenly wishing she had followed her earlier impulse to leave. She knew the women around the table thought she was detached…maybe even thought she was a lesbian. They had no idea she once was like them—dreamy eyed, with an open door to her heart, waiting for the right man to walk through. And he had.

James had romanced her and cajoled her into falling head over heels in love with him. So much so that on Valentine's Day eight years ago, she'd garnered her strength and proposed to *him*. But instead of the wholehearted "yes" she'd expected, the day had gone horribly wrong, shattering her hopes and dreams. Since that day, she'd kept her heart and body carefully under wraps.

When her chest squeezed painfully, Carol gave herself a mental shake, surprised that the mortification of that day still felt so fresh. She dropped her gaze to her feet to gather herself.

That was when she noticed a small white

envelope sticking out of one of the books in her red tote.

Being the long-time employee of a greeting card company, she was accustomed to finding cards in her briefcase and scattered around her car and condo—samples and mockups and overruns. But this card was sealed and seemed to have been placed purposely. She glanced up to see if any of the other women had noticed, but they were congratulating Gabrielle and talking amongst themselves. Ignoring her.

Carol removed the envelope, then slid her thumb under the flap, broke the seal and slid out the card.

The front of the greeting card was a photograph of an early spring scene, with the green shoots of bulb flowers poking through the earth. In the foreground, one large, lone icicle glistened spectacularly. She opened the card and read the computer-generated words inside.

Spring came, and still Carol Snow refused to thaw.

There was no signature.

Hurt whipped through her, leaving her skin

stinging. She knew she had a reputation at work for being cold, knew that people saw her as unfeeling and rigid. Her mind raced, scanning the faces and names of coworkers, wondering which one had gone to the trouble of putting the note in her book...

And her mind stopped on Luke Chancellor, the cad. The reason he'd detained her today wasn't to talk about bonuses—he'd been looking for an opportunity to plant the card. It made even more sense when she recalled his parting shot.

Instead of reading about life, you should try the real thing sometime!

Tears pressed the back of her eyes and she must have uttered something because suddenly, all heads turned in her direction.

"Carol, did you say something?" Page asked.

They all stared at her expectantly, silently challenging her to step up, to join their sexually active sisterhood. Her reluctance to participate in the seduction experiment was like an elephant in the room. In the beginning, she had justified to herself that she barely knew the other women and therefore, owed them no explanation.

But over the course of the monthly meetings, things had changed. Carol felt closer to these women than to anyone else in her life, and she wanted to fit in, wanted to be accepted. Her pleasure over Gabrielle's simple, thoughtful text message in the parking lot was proof that she needed these women and these meetings.

Judging from her traitorous response to Luke Chancellor today, she conceded she would benefit from the physical release a seduction would provide. But if she seduced a man, it wouldn't be with stars in her eyes…it would be purely for revenge. Revenge for the way men had treated her, especially James, but there had been others who had made her feel powerless… men like Luke…

It would serve the cad right if she seduced him and then cast him aside…play the playboy.

"Are you okay?" Cassie asked her in a gentle tone.

Carol wet her lips and nodded. "I've been thinking…"

Eyes widened in her direction, shoulders leaned. Her bravado fled, leaving a trail of perspiration trickling between her breasts.

"Yes, Carol?" Gabrielle prompted in the ensuing silence. "What's on your mind?"

Her heart galloped in her chest, but she managed a smile. "I've decided to try the seduction experiment."

Congratulations reverberated in the room and happy smiles wreathed the faces of her fellow book club members. They seemed equally pleased and surprised. She wondered how their expressions would change if she told them she planned to use sex to avenge her wounded pride, to humiliate, and hopefully, to inflict pain on her target. Only Gabrielle seemed reserved for some reason, studying Carol over the brim of her wine glass. Carol couldn't meet the woman's gaze.

"So who's the lucky guy?" Wendy asked, practically bouncing up and down in her chair.

"Someone I work with," Carol responded casually. "His name is Luke."

"He sounds sexy," Jacqueline said with a smile.

"He's perfect," Carol agreed through gritted teeth. Beneath the table, she crumpled the icicle card into a tight ball in her fist. Too late, she realized Gabrielle had noticed. When she met the woman's gaze, Carol saw the flash of something in the coordinator's eye—apprehension?

"A seduction just in time for Valentine's Day," Cassie continued, oblivious to the exchange, as were the other women. "Do you have a plan?"

"Not really," Carol admitted. "Although… there is the possibility of a company party on the horizon."

"Sounds promising," Wendy said with a grin. "Maybe you and Luke can slip away to a supply closet."

The women laughed and passed around the almond cookies that Carol had brought. For the first time, she felt at ease with her fellow book club members. As the evening progressed and they discussed titles for upcoming selections, she contributed to the discussion and felt accepted. But she was aware of Gabrielle's thoughtful gaze on her throughout.

As they left the meeting, Gabrielle walked out into the parking lot with her. Their breath formed frosty puffs in the winter air.

"It's really getting cold," the older woman offered. "I heard rumors of snow flurries."

Carol laughed. "I think the groceries get that rumor started every year so people will go out and buy milk and bread. It never snows in Atlanta."

Gabrielle nodded, then seemed to turn inward. "I confess your about-face on the seduction experiment surprises me. If you don't me asking, why did you change your mind?"

Carol attempted a casual shrug. Inside her coat pocket, she clenched the crumpled card so hard her hand hurt. "Does it really matter?"

"No," the coordinator admitted. "Just be careful with your motivations, else you might be the person who winds up getting hurt."

"That's not going to happen," Carol assured her.

Gabrielle smiled. "Then I feel sorry for Luke."

As the woman walked away, Carol adopted a smug smile. Someone should feel sorry for Luke. Because, just like the cartoon Cupid dressed in fatigues on the sappy valentine, Carol planned to take no prisoners.

3

Carol sat in her car in the parking lot in front of her office building gripping the cold steering wheel with sweaty hands. She glanced at her watch, fighting the compulsion to go inside. At 7:50 a.m. she was usually well into her workday, but Luke Chancellor always cut it close, so…

As if she had conjured him up, his pewter-colored BMW zipped into view. She followed his car in her rearview mirror, noting where he parked. Then she timed her exit from her own sensible sedan so they would meet on their way into the building. It was a brisk winter morning, with enough of a breeze to send chills up her skirt. Carol tried to ignore the cold, slowing to allow Luke to catch up with her. He was whistling under his breath and tying a yellow tie, his white shirt collar flipped up. When he saw her, he did a double-take and rolled his wrist to check his watch.

"Good morning, Snow," he said with a grin. "Two more minutes and you'd have gotten a tardy slip."

"Good morning, Chancellor," Carol returned as nicely as she could manage given the fact that she wanted to confront him about the icicle card he'd stuck in her book.

"How was your book club?"

"Fine," she said, wondering if the man was, on top of everything else, a mind reader. Her heart pounded in her chest. Could he tell something was different?

"Something's different," he said, looking her up and down.

She stiffened. "What?"

"You're wearing a skirt," he said, appraising her legs. "Nice."

It wasn't that she didn't appreciate the compliment—it was just that she hadn't received a compliment from a man in so long, she didn't know how to respond. "Thank...you?"

He angled his head at her. "Was that a question?"

Flustered, Carol nodded to his undone collar. "Didn't have time to dress at home?"

"Maybe I wasn't at home this morning."

She started to roll her eyes at his insinuation that he'd spent the night elsewhere, then remembered some of the coaching tips the women in the book club had given her—act interested...make eye contact...flirt...touch him...

"So...um...where were you?" she asked, batting her lashes.

"At the gym." Luke squinted. "Do you have something in your eye?"

"Er, yes," she lied, lifting her knuckle for a fake rub.

"Let me see," he said, stopping to turn toward her.

Caught off guard by his sudden proximity, she inhaled sharply, breathing in the scent of shaving cream and soap that emanated from him. Even with her wearing heels, he stood a head taller. The ends of his dark hair were still damp, conjuring up images of him in the gym shower…sudsing sweat from his long, muscular body. He peered into her perfectly healthy eye while she stood stock still in an effort to ward off the sexual vibes rolling off him.

It didn't work. Even standing in the cold wind, her temperature raised a few degrees.

"Hm," he murmured. "I don't see anything. Wait a minute—there's something."

She cut her gaze to him. "What?"

He pulled back. "A pair of big, gorgeous green eyes."

She wanted to scoff, but the sound came out sounding like…a sigh! Then Carol remembered she was *supposed* to be swooning over him. The sheer push-pull of emotion left her paralyzed.

Luke, meanwhile, seemed to be enjoying himself. He walked ahead, his stride carefree. She shook herself and trotted to keep up as they walked into the lobby of the office building. An elevator car was waiting, open. Luke stepped inside, then looked to her. "Are you coming, or are you taking the stairs?"

He was mocking her now. And she was so nervous, Carol was halfway ready to make a run for the stairwell. Maybe this seduction plan wasn't such a good idea after all. Standing next to him in the open air was unnerving enough… she wasn't sure she was ready to be confined with him on the elevator…alone.

Then another woman stepped past her onto the elevator. The cute brunette with the stylish razor-cut hairstyle worked in marketing, Carol recalled. The woman flashed a toothy smile at Luke and the door started to close. At the last second, Carol put out her hand and the door bounced back. She stepped inside and faced the front. When the doors closed, Carol glanced at her reflection, realizing there was nothing "cute" about the way she wore her coarse, bronze-colored hair clasped at the nape of her neck.

This seduction thing was making her self-conscious.

"Luke, do you have plans for Valentine's?" the young woman asked in a hopeful voice.

"Dinner with a special lady," he quipped.

Carol could practically feel the air whoosh

out of the brunette's sails, and she conceded a blip of dismay herself that Luke was dating someone, yet still flirting indiscriminately. Her mouth tightened. All the more reason to bring him down a notch.

At the next floor, the brunette got off, leaving them alone for the ride up another ten floors. Then, to her dismay, Luke reached forward to push the button for every floor in between.

"*What* are you doing?" she demanded.

"Just wanted a couple of minutes to finish tying my tie," he said easily, reaching up to resume the job. "Not sure I'll ever understand why men wear these things."

The elevator doors opened at the next floor and a woman walking past peered inside at the couple, giving them a strange look when neither one of them alighted. When the doors closed, Carol glared at Luke.

"People are going to talk about us."

"It'll do wonders for your reputation… and mine," he said amiably. "It's a win-win situation."

Carol felt a sputter coming on, then reminded herself that she was supposed to be flirting with the man. The elevator climbed, opening and closing on every floor before proceeding. After lying in wait for him in the parking lot, Carol knew she should be taking advantage of this time alone with Luke, but she didn't know what to say.

"How'd I do?" he asked, pulling on the tie.

She glanced over and couldn't help smiling at the crooked knot. "It's lopsided."

"Help me out, Snow?"

When Carol stepped closer, she was struck with a sense of déjà vu she'd always helped James with his ties. That had been so long ago, did she even remember what to do? The size of the knot went in and out of fashion and there was something about putting a dimple in the knot.

The pure silk of Luke's mustard-colored tie felt velvety to her trembling fingers. Beneath the layers of clothing, she could feel the beat of his heart. The electric impulse seemed to transfer to her fingertips and up her arm as she adjusted the knot. She met his dark gaze and for a split second, she thought she saw the same look of surprised confusion she felt fluttering in her stomach. But in a blink, the look was replaced with a teasing light.

"The thought of you reading those naughty books kept me awake last night. It makes me think there's more to you than meets the eye."

His rumbling voice skated over her nerves like sandpaper, stirring responses long-buried in her womb. Carol bit her tongue to keep from asking what the woman he was taking to Valentine's Day dinner would think of that remark, reminding herself that if she was going to seduce this man who had come to represent the Cheating Everyman, she was going to have to pretend that she liked him.

She smoothed her hand down his chest, feeling the wall of muscle beneath his shirt, then conjured up a seductive smile. "You're like a barking dog chasing a car, Chancellor. What would you do if you actually caught it?"

His jaw went slack as the doors to the elevator dinged and opened onto her floor.

"See you at the directors' meeting," she said, then turned on her heel and walked away.

She was pretty sure he was still staring at her when the doors closed.

Carol exhaled slowly. She'd anticipated the nervousness and the awkwardness of being sexually assertive. What she hadn't planned on was the sense of sheer feminine power that filled her chest. It spurred her on to prove to Luke Chancellor that she wasn't the chunk of ice he'd accused her of being.

She would set him on fire, then leave him to burn down.

"Are you okay, Ms. Snow?"

Carol turned at the sound of her assistant Tracy's voice. "Good morning. Yes, I'm fine. Why do you ask?"

"Because you're late," the young redhead said, narrowing her eyes.

"I'm not late."

"It's late for you. And you're flushed. Are you feeling ill?"

Carol straightened. "I'm fine. Did you revise the memo we talked about?"

"It's on your desk." Tracy followed her into her office. "Would you like some coffee?"

Carol set down her briefcase and looked up

with surprise—Tracy had never offered to get her coffee before. "That would be nice, actually, since I'm on my way to a meeting."

"The directors' meeting, yes, I know," Tracy said. "There's a rumor that the company might give out bonuses this year!"

Carol frowned. "You shouldn't listen to watercooler gossip. The idea hasn't even been brought before the directors yet. And even if comes up, it would have to be a unanimous decision."

Looking contrite, Tracy retreated to the lobby. Carol glanced out her office door into the large bullpen area that housed the employees that made up her department. Many people were standing and talking over their cubicles, their body language excited. Carol cursed Luke Chancellor under her breath—no doubt, he'd gotten the rumor started, hoping that employees would pressure their bosses to approve the bonuses. It was the height of irresponsibility, a move meant to make him look good. And it put her between a rock and a hard place.

If she were going to seduce the man, she needed to cozy up to him. But could she set aside her business principles and support his self-indulgent campaign simply to get her ultimate revenge?

Carol skimmed the memo that Tracy had revised, shaking her head when she spied two new typos. She circled them with a red marker, grabbed a pad and pen, then exited her office.

"Here's your coffee, Ms. Snow...you take it black, don't you?"

"Yes, thank you." Carol took the cup, then handed over the memo. "Try again, Tracy...I'd like to see a clean copy on my desk by the time I get back from the meeting."

Tracy bit her lip. "Yes, ma'am."

As Carol strode past the offices of her employees, she noticed their animated chatter quieted. They shot furtive glances in her direction and talked behind their hands. She resented the hell out of Luke for raising the hopes of her employees, and was still feeling rankled when she walked into the boardroom where all of the other eight directors had gathered, with one notable exception—Luke. The group had left the chairs at both ends of the table empty.

By unspoken consent, one chair was reserved for the person who ran the monthly meeting, and the other was reserved for their hero Luke, who would stroll in late, as always.

Since it was Carol's turn to run the meeting, she took one of the chairs and made small talk with her peers, glancing at the agenda that had been passed out. Luke was scheduled to give a sales briefing, but there was no mention of bonuses. Still, just in the couple of minutes since she'd arrived, she'd heard the word whispered and bandied about in conversation.

The man had his own viral marketing posse.

"Shall we get started?" Carol asked.

"Shouldn't we wait on Luke?" Teresa Maitlin, Director of Marketing asked. There were rumors that she and Luke had dated… or something. Luke did seem to be aware of the dangers and legalities of workplace dating and only consorted with women on his level. As Carol looked around the table, she realized she might be the only single female director he hadn't been linked with romantically. She idly wondered if one of these women was his date for Valentine's Day.

"No," Carol said pointedly, then glanced across the table to another member of the Luke Chancellor loved-him-and-lost-him fan club. "Janet, you're up first to give us an update from the Art Department."

Janet took the floor and passed around samples of cards Mystic Touch would be unrolling later in the year for Halloween, Thanksgiving and Christmas. "We're expanding on designs that have proven customer appeal, including military themes and pop culture themes like music." Janet glanced at the still-empty chair. "I'm sure Luke will fill you in on the top sellers of the season."

Carol made a rueful noise. "I'm sure he will, if he ever gets here."

"Something must have come up," someone offered.

"Right. And the rest of us aren't busy," Carol said drily. They moved down the agenda until it was time for Luke to take the floor and he was still a no-show.

"Guess that's a wrap," Carol said, grateful

to dismiss before the idea of bonuses was even raised.

Then the door burst open and a huge bouquet of red heart-shaped helium balloons were shepherded in by a set of long legs that Carol recognized with a sinking feeling. Everyone laughed as Luke went around the room passing out the playful balloons.

Carol accepted one reluctantly, knowing she and everyone else was being manipulated. Luke faced her and gave her a private wink that made her want to strangle him with the ribbon on the balloon she held.

"Doesn't it feel good to get something unexpected?" Luke addressed the room.

While Carol tried not to roll her eyes, everyone chorused agreement.

"And as a greeting card company, isn't that what we're all about? The joy of receiving something unexpected?"

His adoring fans cheered. Carol could only stare at the spectacle. The man was a hypnotist.

"Which is why," he continued with a magnanimous grin, "I propose that we have an impromptu company party this Friday afternoon to celebrate Valentine's Day, our biggest sales day of the year. Since it's not tied to a religious holiday, we don't have to worry about offending anyone, or being politically correct—our employees can just have fun."

From the nods and smiles, Carol knew the party was a done deal. And secretly, she thought it could be fun, although the pragmatist in her would not be quieted.

"As long as we set a reasonable budget," she said.

Luke smiled at her. "I thought I'd leave that to the Director of Finance. And while we're at it, I'd like to suggest that we pay every employee a one thousand dollar bonus."

Carol gasped and any feelings of conflict she'd been having about supporting Luke's idea and seducing him evaporated. "A half million in bonuses? That's outrageous."

"Anything less would be an insult," Luke countered. "We've had a record sales year."

"For one year in a row!" Carol exclaimed. "Next year could be a different story altogether. Wouldn't it be better to take that money and invest in a new high speed color printer, or a state-of-the-art cutter? My department would benefit from new computers on everyone's desk. Or maybe we could kick in more on our employees' health care premiums?"

Luke shook his head. "That's not tangible. Why not give our workers the money so they can spend it however they see fit?"

"Because it's not a prudent investment," Carol said, crossing her arms. Which would've been more menacing if the movement hadn't made the helium heart-shaped balloon bump her in the nose. She slapped at the balloon and lost a grip on the ribbon. It rose to the ceiling where it hit a hot light and burst.

Everyone jumped.

"Now then," Carol continued, "I agree the idea of a company party has merit—if we did something on-site, it could be affordable, and something that everyone could enjoy. But I'm not convinced that employee bonuses are the best way to spend a half million dollars."

Janet bit her lip and shrugged at Luke. "Carol has a point, Luke. The vote has to be unanimous, and when it comes to financial matters, I'll always follow Carol's lead."

Luke nodded, then clapped his hands. "Since we all agree on a party, why don't we move ahead with those plans, and take some time to think about the bonuses."

Carol narrowed her eyes. Meaning, take some time for him to *campaign for support for the bonuses.*

"We could reconvene Friday morning," he said, then he cut his gaze to Carol. "If we reached an agreement that morning to pay a bonus, could we have the checks printed in time to give to employees at the party that afternoon?"

Carol pursed her mouth. "*If* we reached an agreement, it would be possible, I suppose."

"Okay," Luke said with a grin. "Let's have a party!"

As the meeting broke up, Carol marveled how everyone gravitated to Luke. He was animated as he spoke to Teresa, the Director of Marketing, whose team handled employee events and would be coordinating the party. Carol flashed back to this morning when she had straightened Luke's tie on the elevator. For a few seconds, she had detected something between them, and for a few moments, had been almost...*excited* about the prospect of seducing him. Standing here, she conceded a little disappointment that even though she knew she'd made the right business decision for her conscience, she would occasionally think about what might have been. Sure, she'd been planning to dump him after the seduction...but it might've been fun along the way...

Then Luke lifted his gaze to hers and over the heads of their peers, the proprietary look in his eyes sent an arrow of longing straight to her sex. She was reminded of the "take no prisoners" Cupid dressed in camouflage because Luke was looking at her as if she were the hill on which he was going to plant his flag.

She knew that look: Luke was planning to change her mind about the employee bonuses. The question was, how far would she let him go to win her over?

By standing up to him, she'd flipped the seduction production. Now who was seducing whom?

4

The next morning, Thursday, Carol pulled into the parking lot at her regular time, so early that only the security guards were working. But she spied another car in the parking lot—a pewter-colored BMW—and smirked when she saw Luke emerge and hurry in her direction, smothering a yawn. She had to give him points for getting up with the birds to start trying to win her over.

It was a frosty, still morning, cold enough to sting her nose and eyes. Carol lifted her gaze toward the rising sun to find an eerie, reddish hue bleeding over the horizon. The strange color of the winter sky left her with a sense of foreboding that enveloped her this time every year. A shiver skated down her spine. She couldn't wait to put another Valentine's Day behind her.

Her phone chimed to let her know a text message had arrived. She slowed to unclip it from her purse and glanced at the screen. It was from Gabrielle Pope.

Sensing all is not well, hope I'm wrong…let me know if I can help.

Carol squinted. How could Gabrielle possibly know that something had derailed her seduction of Luke?

The man himself bounded up next to her. "Good morning, Snow."

Flustered by the text message from Gabrielle, Carol was further dismayed by the way her vital signs spiked at the sight of Luke in his charcoal gray suit, white shirt, and lime-green-colored tie. Carol vaguely wondered what kind of outdoor activity kept the man so tan and virile-looking.

And when she had become so susceptible to his physical endowments.

"Is that an early morning message from your lover?" he asked, peering at her phone.

She yanked it to her chest. "No."

"No message, or no lover?" he teased.

Carol frowned. "You're early, Chancellor."

He smiled. "That's because I couldn't sleep last night thinking about you, Snow."

She pursed her mouth. "Don't you get tired of using that line?"

His eyes danced. "More specifically, thinking about what you said in the meeting yesterday about your department needing new computers. I might have a solution."

She glanced at him sideways as he held open the door for her. "I'm listening."

"It's better if I show you," he said as they walked to the elevator. When she gave him a suspicious look, he grinned. "Trust me."

Carol averted her gaze. She didn't trust him, or herself. Damn the whole seduction by the book exercise that Gabrielle had proposed. Before the book club, Carol had been content with her sexless life. She'd focused her energy on her career and convinced herself she didn't need a man. But once the idea of seducing Luke had been planted, the sexy man had hijacked her thoughts and her dreams.

As a reminder of his disdain for her, she fingered the crumpled icicle card that she'd left in her coat pocket. If he was being nice to her, it was simply because he wanted her to support the idea of paying bonuses when it came up again at the directors' meeting tomorrow morning.

Men. Could. Not. Be. Trusted.

After they walked onto the elevator, he pushed the button for the basement.

"Where are you taking me?" she asked.

"You'll see," he said with a wink.

He was so casual, so confident. The man never carried a briefcase or a laptop, she noticed irritably. By comparison, she felt like the B student who took every book home every night next to the straight-A student who never studied.

The short elevator ride seemed interminably long. Carol looked up, then down, anywhere to avoid looking at Luke…and noticing the way his suit jacket perfectly outlined his broad shoulders.

"So, did you curl up in bed with a book last night?" he asked.

Her mouth tightened. "Why are you interested in my bedtime reading material?"

"I'm interested in everything about you,
Carol, but you're not the easiest person to get
to know."

Her head came up and she looked at him.
He sounded almost...*sincere*. His gaze was
intense. "Forget the books you're reading," he
said quietly. "What's *your* story? Why are you
so prickly?"

She bristled—who was he to judge her? "Just
because I'm immune to your charms, Chancellor, doesn't mean there's something wrong with
me."

He leaned in close, until she could see the
thick fringe of his dark lashes. "I don't think
you're as immune as you let on, Snow. Your
lips say one thing, but the color in your cheeks
says something else entirely."

"You don't know what you're talking about,"
Carol said, but her denial sounded thin, even to
her ears. Her cheeks flamed. When the elevator
doors opened, she practically fell out to escape
his company. She willed her pulse to slow, her
breasts and thighs to ignore the pheromones

the man emitted indiscriminately, like Johnny Appleseed.

"This is where we're having the party, by the way," he said as they stepped into a large open area. At the far end of the space sat offices of personnel who supervised the enormous printers and other pieces of computer equipment housed in the basement. Through their office window, someone threw up their hand and Luke waved back. He seemed to have the run of the place.

Carol followed him as he turned and walked down a dark hallway that seemed to lead nowhere. "Are you planning to off me so the directors will approve bonuses?"

His laughter boomed into the empty space. "No. I have a better plan." He stopped and flipped on a light that revealed a nondescript door. On a small keyboard, he punched in a code that triggered a click, then he pushed open the door. "After you," he said, rolling his hand to indicate she was to precede him.

Carol was skeptical, but curiosity won out. She stepped toward the large supply room filled with miscellaneous furniture and computer equipment.

And it was *nice* stuff—wood desks and credenzas, glass-front bookcases, flat-screen monitors and CPU towers and sleek laptops. There were leather desk chairs, color printers, scanners, wireless keyboards, web cameras, and more.

She walked inside to survey the rows and rows of furniture and laden shelves. He followed her and the heavy door swung closed behind them.

"What is this place?" she asked.

"It's where leftovers and trade-ins are stored."

"But where did it all come from?"

"Mostly from the sales team in the field."

Her jaw dropped. "Everything in here gathering dust is nicer than the furniture and equipment my employees work on every day! Why didn't I know about his room?"

"You do…now."

She set down her briefcase and purse, gazing around in awe. "What is this, some sort of company secret?"

"I wouldn't call it a secret," he said, hedging. "Technically, all this equipment belongs to the sales department."

She knew better than anyone that sales got the lion's share of the administrative budget—a budget that had gone up steeply since Luke had become director. To attract the best talent, he'd convinced the executive committee to allocate more funds for commissions and perks, like state-of-the-art computers and deep expense accounts. True, the expenditures had proved to be a good investment, but it also left other employees feeling resentful. Carol set her jaw.

"So did you just bring me down here to rub it in?"

Luke turned toward her and she realized suddenly how vulnerable she was with him in here…alone. She wasn't afraid of him, just afraid of her reaction to him. At his nearness, her breathing became shallow, and her nipples budded. She was grateful that her winter coat hid her responses, but the way he looked at her, as if he knew the effect he had on her, was unnerving. His previous comment that her body language betrayed her made her feel even more exposed.

"Where would you like for me to rub it in?" he murmured.

Carol tried to rally an indignant reply, but she couldn't seem to form the angry words. Not even when he planted his hands on either side of her, effectively caging her between the shelf at her back and his big body. Instead, it was as if the will to resist him leaked out of her body. Carol lifted her gaze slowly, over his broad chest and up his crooked tie to the square chin, past the sensual mouth and strong nose to those incredible brown eyes that seemed to pull at her. She reasoned that the equipment in the room must be emitting electrical charges because the scant air between their bodies fairly crackled.

She realized he was going to kiss her, and she didn't want to stop him. As his mouth moved toward hers and his features softened, she told herself she'd planned to seduce him, hadn't she? What did it matter who was on top and who—

Suddenly Luke pulled back with a blanched

expression. "I'm sorry, I—" He straightened and wiped his hand over his mouth. "Carol, I don't know what came over me. It's like—" He looked around the room as if he just realized where they were, then he stepped back and looked her over. "Are you okay?"

She nodded as anger whipped through her. "I'm fine, Chancellor. Is this where you bring all your conquests?"

"What? Of course not. I've never—" He stopped and put out his hands. "I apologize—I lost my head." He cleared his throat and seemed to collect himself. "Are we good?"

Carol burned with humiliation that she'd wanted that kiss so much. She should be grateful that Luke had had the restraint to pull away. Instead she was left with the sensation of having something stolen from her. Old feelings of rejection zoomed to the surface, staggering her. She stuck her shaking hands in the pockets of her coat and found the crumpled card, another reminder that Luke was toying with her, and she'd fallen for it.

"Are you going to tell me why you brought me here?" she said through gritted teeth.

He scratched his temple as if he'd forgotten. "I was going to help you, um, liberate, whatever equipment your department needs."

Carol hesitated. Her first instinct—especially now—was to refuse anything he offered. But the practical side of her couldn't deny that her employees deserved nice equipment, and she understood office politics. Luke had something she needed and was gifting it to her. She wasn't going to side with him on the matter of the employee bonuses, but why not get something for her people in the meantime?

"Okay," she said. "How do we do this?"

"Today I have to help get things ready for tomorrow's party. Meet me back here after hours?"

Warning bells sounded in her head. After hours…alone…in a confined space. *Danger! Danger!*

Luke lifted his hands. "I promise to be on my best behavior."

"Okay," Carol heard herself say. And that tightness in her chest over his pronouncement to behave himself, was that relief—or disappointment?

5

No matter how hard Carol tried to keep her mind and hands busy and off the after-hours meeting with Luke, the workday crawled by. Conversely, her body hummed with restless energy. She told herself it was the nervous excitement of doing something unorthodox when it came to shuffling company assets. But Luke's near-kiss this morning had haunted her all day—she could almost taste his lips on hers. Why had he suddenly grown a conscience? Obviously, she was going to have to take control if this seduction thing was going to happen. She would sleep with him once, and because she was now so well-read on erotic love play, she would make sure it was the hottest encounter of his life. And when the moment was right, she'd let him know she knew it was him who'd planted the icicle card and tell him to get lost.

At long last, the clock on her desk flipped to five o'clock. Already wearing her coat and with briefcase in hand, Carol walked out of her office.

Her assistant Tracy's eyebrows shot up. "You're going home?"

"That's right," Carol said, biting her tongue to keep from telling her assistant she didn't have to explain herself.

"It's only five o'clock. Did someone die?"

Carol pressed her lips together. "No." She handed Tracy the latest version of the memo, this time with four errors circled in red. "Again, please."

Tracy sighed. "Yes, ma'am."

Carol looked to the bullpen where her employees worked on dated computers, some of which were shared. A situation she hoped to remedy soon. Before she turned away, she noticed people glaring in her direction, then exchanging knowing looks with each other. Now that she thought about it, her employees had maintained a wide arc around her all day…

She turned back to her assistant. "Tracy, is there something going on I should know about?"

The young redhead worked her mouth back and forth, obviously weighing whether to be truthful. "Well…word around the watercooler is you're standing in the way of everyone getting bonuses."

Carol's shoulders fell when she realized the collective hostility being directed toward her. She was surprised how much the knowledge hurt, and it made her tone sharp. "I believe a better use of the money is reinvesting in the company. In the long run, we'll all benefit more."

Tracy's mouth tightened into a bow. "I'll have the revised memo on your desk in the morning, Ms. Snow."

"Thank you. Good night."

As Carol walked out, she felt the heat of angry stares boring into her. But as a senior money manager for the company, it was her job to make unpopular decisions. Hopefully the new equipment would help to alleviate ill will.

She braved the notorious Atlanta rush-hour traffic and passed the time taking in the magnificent, brooding color palette of the sky— reds and oranges. An omen of bad weather? Whatever the cause, it was unsettling to her for a reason she couldn't put her finger on.

At home she undressed and redressed slowly, studying her slight curves with a critical eye, something she hadn't done in quite a while. She'd gotten talked into a couple of blind dates in the years since she and James had split, but she hadn't been intimate with anyone. When the moment of truth arrived with Luke, she hoped she remembered what to do.

One thing was certain—she'd be drawing heavily on her recent reading material for the Red Tote Book Club.

The text message from Gabrielle suddenly slid into Carol's mind. She hadn't responded, and now felt compelled to, if only to circumvent the well-meaning woman from interfering. Pulling out her phone, Carol used the touch pad to type in: *Thanks for your concern, but everything going as planned.*

She hit Send and bit her lip at the white lie, but she knew Gabrielle well enough to know that the woman would worry otherwise.

When she drove back to the office at the prescribed meet time, Carol felt like a thief, stealing into the building after most people had gone home. She waved to the guard, then rode the elevator down to the basement. When she alighted, the cavernous space was darker than it had been this morning. Lights in only half of the offices across the way were burning. She could barely see to walk.

"Luke?" she whispered. "Are you here?" She turned and bumped into a wall…with arms. She stumbled backward, but he reached out and steadied her.

"I got you," he murmured close to her ear.

"Why didn't you say something?" she snapped.

"I thought if I was quiet, you might grope around a little."

Her eyes were starting to adjust to the darkness, allowing her to see the light of mischief in his gaze. Her body softened in secret places, leaving her feeling exposed. He was teasing her, and she was bending like putty.

"Shouldn't we get started?" she asked, trying to regain the upper hand.

"Yes," he said, sounding like a little boy who'd been reprimanded. "This way."

He clasped her hand, then led her down the hallway. His fingers felt warm and strong around hers, sending her mind leaping in directions of how it would feel to have his hands on her naked body. Carol felt along the wall with her free hand. "Can we turn on a light?"

"I'd rather not draw attention to our little mission."

She followed him until he stopped. He released her hand to punch in the key code and then a click sounded. Luke reclaimed her hand and guided her into the room, and when the door closed, turned on banks of lights to illuminate the room.

As Carol blinked against the glare, Luke emitted a low whistle. When he came into focus, she realized he was looking at her. "You let your hair down. I like it."

She combed her fingers through the unruly layers self-consciously. "Thanks."

"And wow, I don't think I've ever seen you in anything except a suit, Snow. Nice."

She wore black jeans, black turtleneck, black bomber jacket and black boots. Satisfaction curled in her chest over his compliment, although she tried not to react. "Contrary to popular belief, I have a wardrobe and a life outside the office." She nodded to his clothing. "You look more comfortable than the last time I saw you."

In truth, Luke looked breathtakingly handsome in dark jeans, rugged athletic shoes, and a red V-neck sweater over a white T-shirt. He smiled and nodded, then leaned forward. "Interesting earrings."

"Thanks." Carol reached up to stroke the dangling sterling cylinders that featured channel-set emeralds. James had given them to her.... He'd said emeralds were the "stone of successful love." What a load of manure. She'd worn them tonight as a reminder that men couldn't be trusted. She would use Luke to get what her employees needed, but she had no illusions as to his motivations for helping her.

"Did you bring a list?" he asked.

She pulled a rolled sheaf of papers from her coat pocket. "An inventory of the equipment in my department, and a wish list."

Luke unrolled the pages and scanned them. "Okay, let's start with the wish list. One color laser printer."

At that point, it became a scavenger hunt. The two of them walked the aisles between shelves, looking for something to fit the bill. If one of them found it, they shouted out, and the item got tagged. It was almost fun, Carol conceded. She found herself looking for glimpses of Luke as he moved between shelving units. Damn, the man could wear a pair of jeans.

"So tell me about this life you have outside of work," he called.

She hesitated, but being obscured by the cluttered shelves made her feel safe. "I like to cook."

"Will you marry me?"

She blinked, then leaned into the open aisle. "Huh?"

Down a few rows, Luke leaned into the aisle, too, and flashed a grin. "Kidding." His head disappeared. "Keep going. What do you like about cooking?"

Carol pulled back and toyed with a wireless computer mouse on the shelf in front of her. "I guess I like all the things that go along with it. In the summer I have a small organic plot in the community garden at Piedmont Park."

"Cool. What do you grow?"

"Nothing fancy—corn and beans, peppers and tomatoes."

"Gotta love home-grown tomatoes," came his muffled reply.

"Food seems to taste better when you've grown it yourself," she agreed. "But I like shopping for food, too."

"I make a trip to the Dekalb Farmers Market a couple of times a month," he said.

Impressed, Carol pursed her mouth. "You do?"

"Best selection of international beers in the area."

She laughed. "That's true, I guess."

He appeared at the end of the shelf where

she stood. "So, who gets to enjoy the fruits of your labor?"

Caught off guard by his sudden proximity, Carol blinked. "Huh?"

"Who do you cook for?"

She averted her gaze and pretended to scrutinize something higher on the shelf. "Oh…you know—friends and…stuff." Nobody.

"No family close by?"

She shook her head and chanced a glance in his direction. "I don't have any family left. My parents are gone and I'm an only child."

Sympathy flashed in his dark eyes. "I'm sorry."

Carol shrugged. "Thanks, but I've been on my own for a while."

"It makes me feel guilty for all the times I've wanted peace and quiet from my family."

"You have a big one?"

"Three sisters, two brothers, assorted nieces and nephews, and my folks are still alive and well."

Envy coursed through her. "That must make for big holiday gatherings."

He nodded. "It's chaos."

It sounded heavenly to her, but she didn't comment.

He disappeared again, then called out that he'd found another item on the list. Carol crossed it off her copy.

"Ever been married, Snow?"

Her head came up at his question even though from the sound of his voice, he was on the other side of the room. James's face appeared in her mind and her face burned with shame. "No. You?"

"No. Have you ever been close?"

"Not really," she said. "You?"

"No."

Since he couldn't see her, Carol smirked. Meaning he wasn't serious about the "special lady" he was taking out for Valentine's Day dinner? No big surprise.

Even though he'd brought it up, the topic of committed relationships seemed to have soured him on conversation for a while because he lapsed into silence as he turned on machines to ensure they were operational.

They made multiple trips up and down aisles, opened boxes and sorted through bins of miscellaneous equipment. Over the course of a couple of hours, they were able to find about half the equipment on Carol's wish list, and locate newer computers to replace almost all the machines her employees currently used. They were nearing the end of the list when Luke got chatty again.

"So, Snow," he said from some unseen corner, "tell me about this naughty book club of yours."

Carol squirmed. "It's not 'naughty.' We read and discuss classic erotica."

"I stand corrected—it's even dirtier than I thought."

She couldn't help but laugh. "There's nothing dirty about it."

His face suddenly appeared on the other side of the shelving unit where she stood. "Can you let me have my fantasies?"

Her traitorous body surged with longing. Instead of responding, she lifted a device that resembled a gun and pointed it at him. "I found a handheld scanner."

He put his hand over his heart and pretended to stagger back. "You got me. With me gone, you can do whatever you want with the half million dollars."

Carol sighed, remembering the glares from her own employees. "It's not what *I* want, Chancellor—it's what I think is best for the company."

He nodded, his expression congenial. "As long as you're not opposing the bonuses simply because it was my idea."

And just like that, she remembered what a jerk he was. Anger bubbled in her chest—anger at Luke Chancellor, wunderkind, and anger at all the men out there who steamrolled through life, crushing the hopes and the hearts and the careers of anyone who got in their way—after using that person as a means to their own selfish ends. But she reeled in her temper, remembering her personal and professional goals. Luke would get his.

"No," she said quietly, walking closer to brush dust off the shoulder of Luke's red sweater. It was a casual caress, but the warmth of his body reached through the fibers and seeped into her fingers, making them tingle. "In fact, I've decided to keep an open mind when the directors reconvene tomorrow morning to take another vote."

Luke's gaze followed her hand down his sleeve. "You have?"

"Yes."

"That's great." He grinned. "I appreciate your being flexible."

"I take yoga," she offered with a smile. "I'm nothing if not flexible."

She was feeling smug about throwing him off balance, but then the tip of his tongue appeared to wet his lips, sending Carol's imagination running in a different direction. Her midsection tightened. If only Luke wasn't so... orally gifted.

He was staring at her. "So...what now?"

Carol's pulse spiked. Should she make the first move? Kiss him? Tear off his red sweater? Tackle him? Her mind raced back over the erotic books she'd read...the common theme was women taking control of their sexual experiences.

Still...it had been a long time...

"What did you have in mind?" she asked.

"I was thinking it'll take most of the night."

She swallowed hard. A little cocky, yes, but it was hard not to be impressed by his confidence. "P-probably. My place?" She had stocked up on enough body butter to slide through a keyhole and enough condoms to protect a sorority.

Luke gave a little laugh. "Of course your place. If it's alright with you, I'll supervise."

Carol opened her mouth to agree, then narrowed her eyes. "Supervise?"

"To make sure none of the equipment gets broken." He gestured to the flat-screen monitor behind him. "It would be a shame to move all this stuff to your department only for it to be damaged in transit."

Slowly, she realized that she and Luke were having two different conversations. For once, *she* had sex on the brain, *he* was thinking depreciating assets.

"You want to move everything tonight?" she asked.

"I think it would be less likely to raise a red flag if the equipment is already in place when your people get in tomorrow, don't you?"

"Probably."

"Go home," he said. "I'll take care of every-thing. In case someone questions what's going on, I don't want you to get in trouble."

Disappointment that the seduction wouldn't take place tonight was crowded out by an odd feeling—she couldn't remember the last time someone had been *protective* of her. "O…kay."

Warmth and sincerity radiated from Luke's eyes, disorienting her. She'd come tonight with the intention of enticing him, then taking him down a notch. But he'd ruined things by being so…nice. Dammit.

"See you tomorrow?" he said, his eyes crin-kling at the corners.

Carol backed toward the door—she had to get away from those crinkles. "See you tomorrow."

Her pulse clicked at top speed on the way back to her car. She raised her coat collar against the cold and rubbed her hands to-gether briskly. She could *not* be falling for Luke Chancellor…she wouldn't let herself. She drove home with hands planted firmly on the steering wheel, determined to regain control of her emotions. When she arrived at her condo, though, one glance in her foyer mirror confirmed her worst suspicions—bright eyes, pink cheeks and a subtle softening of her mouth… she was succumbing to Luke Chancellor's spell. Dammit.

Then she gasped and her hand flew to her ear. One of her emerald earrings was missing. A low moan of anguish sounded from the back of her throat. She frantically backtracked to her car and looked inside, but didn't find it.

Hot tears flooded Carol's eyes—how fitting that she lose the one nice gift James had given her, the one thing that reminded her to keep her heart in check.

From her belt, her phone chimed to signal an incoming text message. Before she even looked, Carol knew it was from Gabrielle Pope.

Just remember that the best-laid plans often go astray.

Carol closed her eyes. She was obviously the target of some kind of cosmic Valentine's Day conspiracy.

But she would not surrender.

6

Carol wanted to arrive early the next morning so she could see the looks on the faces of her employees when they saw their new computers, but traffic and the elements conspired against her.

The early sky was angry, a spewing volcano of rolling red clouds that seemed to have an adverse effect on morning commuters. Horns punctuated the air as cars inched toward their destination. On the radio, experts and laypersons offered explanations for the phenomenon. The leading theory suggested the recent drought had allowed an extreme amount of dust from Georgia red clay to accumulate in the atmosphere, accounting for the eerie coloring of the clouds. Regardless of the source, Carol longed for blue skies again.

It was a few minutes past eight o'clock when she pulled into the parking lot. A frigid wind cut through her coat and scarf as she hurried into the building. Atlanta almost never got this cold. It felt…unnatural.

Her heart tripped in anticipation as she rode up on the elevator. It felt good to reward her employees and she conceded that she was even rethinking her position on paying out bonuses. Luke had surprised her last night in the supply room with his warmth and interest…maybe she'd been wrong about him and his motives.

When the elevator doors opened, she smiled at the hum of excited voices. She walked into the area, pleased to see the printers and other peripherals had been installed, and "new" laptops sat on everyone's desks. Tracy, caressing her own new computer, turned a beaming smile in Carol's direction. "Look at all this stuff—isn't it wonderful?"

Carol nodded, then opened her mouth with the intention of saying "You're welcome."

"And we have Luke Chancellor to thank for it," Tracy added with a dreamy sigh.

Carol swallowed her words. "Luke Chancellor?"

"Can you believe it? Apparently he was here all night installing refurbished machines he found somewhere."

Carol's mouth puckered. "Really?"

"Everyone in this department has needed new computers for so long—I know you tried and tried to get them requisitioned. Luke must have pulled a lot of strings to make this happen."

Carol pushed her tongue into her cheek. "He pulled something, all right. How do you know it was him?"

"Everyone knows—it's all over the building. And everyone's excited about the party this afternoon. Apparently, that was his idea, too... along with the bonuses." Her assistant gave her a wary look, then held up a sheet of paper. "I gave the memo another stab."

"Thank you," Carol said, plucking it from her assistant's hand.

As she proceeded toward her office, Luke's

name was in the air. Employees parted in her wake, and their expressions of excitement over their new equipment changed to mild disdain when they looked her way. Their message was clear: *Luke Chancellor will do things for us, but you won't.* If she tried to defend herself at this point, it would only look as if she was trying to take credit to save face.

Luke's words from the previous evening came back to her. *Go home…I'll take care of everything. In case someone questions what's going on, I don't want you to get in trouble.*

And to think she'd believed he was being protective.

Heat infused her body as she set down her briefcase and hung up her coat. He'd made a fool out of her. Not only did everyone know that she was the lone holdout when it came to granting bonuses, but he'd managed to make it look as if he cared about her own department more than she did.

Angry tears scalded her eyelids, but she fought mightily to keep them at bay. She didn't want anyone at work to see her break down. She needed to escape for a few minutes to collect herself before the directors' meeting. Carol considered fleeing to the ladies' room, then remembered she needed to look for the missing earring that she'd most likely lost in the equipment room. She could be alone there.

She backtracked to the elevator and did her best to ignore the accusatory glances from people she passed—apparently word had spread quickly. While she waited for a car to arrive, someone muttered "Ice Queen" under their breath disguised as a cough. A few people tittered. Carol's face burned as she walked onto the elevator, but she managed to lift her chin and keep it together on the short ride to the basement.

When the doors opened, she realized that preparations were already underway for the afternoon party. Red decorations of cupids and hearts abounded. Blowups of some of the company's Valentine's Day cards leaned against the wall, including the "take no prisoners" card she'd seen on her assistant's desk. Cupid looked even more menacing at life-size.

Thankfully, she didn't see Luke among the

volunteers…but the people who saw her threw her a look of distaste before turning back to their tasks. Stung, Carol hurried to the stockroom. There she punched in the code she'd seen Luke use and slipped inside.

When the door closed behind her, she leaned against its cool surface for a few seconds, reveling in the quiet. It had been an unsettling week and she fervently wished she could hit the rewind button.

Unfortunately, life didn't come with a remote control.

At length she felt for the light switch and illuminated the room. The shelves were much more bare than yesterday…the equipment scavenged for her department had made a big dent in the inventory. Carol released a pent-up breath and allowed herself the luxury of a few miserable tears.

How had she gotten to this place in her life? She'd thought by now she'd be at the pinnacle of her career, married to a great guy and maybe starting a family. Instead, she felt as if she'd regressed to high school—no matter what she did, no one liked her.

And she was alone. Completely, absolutely, utterly alone.

With no answers at hand, she found a tissue and blew her nose, then began walking up and down the aisles, looking for her missing earring. The longer she walked, the more bitter frustration built up in her chest—frustration toward James, who had so callously toyed with her heart. And toward Luke, who had so easily usurped her authority and conned her with a few probing questions and a handful of compliments.

From the floor, a glint of metal caught her eye. To her relief, it was her silver-and-emerald earring. She knelt to retrieve it from under a shelf, but lost her balance and bumped the shelving unit accidentally. Above her, she heard a scraping noise, and when she looked up, something large was bearing down on her.

Carol didn't have time to put up her hand. Pain exploded in her head, then everything went black.

7

Someone was shaking Carol by the shoulder.

"Ms. Snow...Ms. Snow?"

She opened her eyes to blink her assistant Tracy's face into view, then winced at the pain that stabbed her temple.

"Oh, thank God—she opened her eyes," Tracy said. "Ms. Snow, are you okay?"

Carol sat up and lifted her hand to her head, where a goose egg had formed. "I think so. I leaned over to pick up an earring I lost and something fell on my head."

"That monitor," a young man said, pointing to a boxy computer screen sitting nearby on its end. "You're lucky you weren't killed."

Carol squinted. "Who are you?"

"My boyfriend, Stan," Tracy said. "He works here in the basement and was walking by when he heard a crash. He recognized you and called me. Should I call an ambulance?"

"No," Carol said, gingerly pushing to her feet. "It's just a bump on the head. I'll be fine."

"Are you sure?"

"Of course I'm sure," Carol snapped. "I have a meeting to go to."

Tracy glanced at her watch. "Actually, the directors' meeting has already started."

Carol brushed off her clothes and straightened her lapel. "Then I'd better be going." She glanced at Tracy's boyfriend. "Thank you for coming to my assistance."

Then she marched out, embarrassed to have been in such a compromising situation. She palpated the tender knot on her forehead. A low, throbbing headache had settled into her crown. The pain brought her near tears again, but she was more determined than ever to stand up to Luke Chancellor. After stopping by the ladies' room to arrange her hair over the reddened bump, Carol proceeded to the room where the directors' meeting was being held and pushed open the door.

Her fellow directors looked up and she could tell not all of them were relieved to see her. Luke Chancellor sat at the head of the table. He smiled up at her. "We were just getting ready to send out a search party for you, Carol."

"I'll bet you were," she said sweetly, then settled into an empty chair. "Sorry I'm late."

"We heard a Good Samaritan delivered new computer equipment to your department this morning," Janet, the art director, said with a smile.

All gazes slid toward Luke. He held up his hands. "It was Carol's idea—I just… facilitated."

She set her jaw—how did he do that? Manage to sound humble and still take credit?

"Have you revisited the issue of bonuses?" Carol asked, pulling the conversation back to the matter at hand. She shot a look of contempt in Luke's direction.

He caught her gaze and confusion registered on his face…what an actor.

"We were just about to," Luke said, then

cleared his voice. "I think it's pretty clear that anyone dissenting is following your lead, Carol, so I guess we can cut to the chase by asking if you've changed your mind on the issue of paying out a one-time bonus?"

The weight of a roomful of stares shifted to her. Luke looked hopeful, and Carol knew he was remembering her comment from the previous evening, that she might reconsider her position. But that was when she'd been under the spell he seemed to be able to cast so easily with a handsome face and a few flattering words. That was before he'd made her feel stupid for falling for his caring act, before he'd embarrassed her, turned all her employees against her. This might be her one and only chance to put Luke Chancellor in his place.

"No, I haven't changed my mind. Not about the bonuses, not about a lot of things," she added pointedly.

Disappointment colored Luke's face. His mouth flattened, then he shrugged. "I guess that's that."

"I guess so," Carol chirped, then pushed up from her chair. "If that's all, I really need to get back to work. This party means I have only four hours to get done what I'd normally do in eight."

Luke's mouth tightened. "That's all."

Carol gave him a triumphant look, then walked out. On the way back to her office, she massaged her temples, trying to alleviate the headache that had yet to ease. When she reached her department, she walked the gauntlet of angry stares and closed her office door. There she downed some aspirin and waited for the feeling of vindication to descend. She'd proved to Luke that her opinion still meant something around here…that there was at least one woman he couldn't charm into submission.

But sitting here in the wake of her power, the victory felt strangely hollow. She shook it off, reasoning that she could hardly feel good about anything while nursing a headache. She would savor the success later, in private.

When she was alone. Completely, absolutely, utterly alone.

She pushed away the troubling thought, announced to Tracy through the intercom that she wasn't to be disturbed, then spent the morning plowing through a mountain of paperwork. At some point Carol decided she'd skip the Valentine's Day party and just go home, maybe tuck in with a good book, something she could suggest as a selection for the Red Tote Book Club.

While she was thinking about it, she pulled out her phone and sent a text message to Gabrielle.

Change of plans...seduction OFF.

A couple of minutes later, Gabrielle replied.

Surrender to love, Carol.

Carol frowned at the message. Love? Who said anything about love?

And *surrender?* Never.

A knock sounded at her door, then it creaked open.

"Tracy, I asked not to be disturbed," Carol said without looking up.

"Don't get mad at her," Luke said.

Carol lifted her head to see the man of the hour standing in her doorway. He gestured behind him. "Tracy said you didn't want to be disturbed, but I told her I'd take full responsibility for defying your orders."

He looked handsome in brown slacks and pale blue dress shirt, minus a tie. Her pulse quickened, but she reminded herself that he wasn't to be trusted.

Men. Could. Not. Be. Trusted.

"What do you want, Chancellor?"

"I thought it would be nice if we walked into the party together, a show of solidarity."

She stood and began packing her briefcase. "I'm not going to the party."

He gave a little laugh. "Not going? Why not?"

"Because I'd rather go home, that's why."

"Go home to what?" he asked. "A book?"

At his mocking tone, Carol bit down on the inside of her cheek. "What's it to you?" She looked up and her anger surged to the surface. "I mean, really, Luke, as if you care."

He blinked and visibly pulled back. "That's the thing—I *do* care… Although I'm starting to wonder why."

She rolled her eyes—it was a preposterous statement considering the fact that he'd compared her to an icicle that wouldn't thaw. "Save it, Chancellor. Go." She made a shooing motion. "Go be the life of the party, the company hero, the lady-killer."

She'd spoken with more venom than she'd intended, but once the words were out, she couldn't take them back.

Luke pursed his mouth, then nodded in acquiescence and turned toward the door. She looked back to her briefcase and slammed the lid shut.

"Carol?"

She looked up, surprised he was still standing there. "Yes?"

"I hope you change your mind about the party."

She walked over to her coatrack and shrugged into her coat. "I won't."

"Then maybe fate will intervene." He grinned and strode out.

Carol squinted, then shook her head. Luke could not accept the fact that he couldn't charm her into doing what he wanted.

When she walked out into the lobby area of her department, only Tracy was still there, sitting at her desk obediently, although she glanced longingly at the clock.

"I'm leaving," Carol announced.

"You're not staying for the party?"

"No."

"Is it because your head is hurting?"

At the compassionate tone in her assistant's voice, Carol balked. "Uh…no. But thank you." Then she handed Tracy the perennial memo, riddled with bright red circles. "Six mistakes on this version."

Tracy winced. "Really?"

"Really." Carol gave her a pointed look. "Try again, please."

Tracy bit her lip and nodded. "Be careful driving home. I hear a winter storm is blowing in."

Carol laughed. "I grew up in Atlanta, and none of those so-called 'winter storms' ever materialize. Enjoy the party."

She headed toward the elevator. The offices in every department were empty, with everyone already in the basement for the party. As she rode down to the lobby, Luke's words came floating back to her.

That's the thing—I do care...

Carol shook her head. The man was a master. She knew he was a player, yet she still almost believed him.

The doors opened into the empty lobby. She walked out and headed toward the front entrance. A rumble overhead made her stop. She realized it was a fierce wind shaking the glass of the two-story entryway. The sky looked almost purple—the low-hanging red clouds were brimming with some type of serious precipitation. Rain? Hail?

Neither.

She watched in disbelief as enormous snowflakes exploded from the sky, only to be swept sideways in an almost tornadic wind. Within seconds, the outdoors was enveloped in a thick, impermeable blur of white.

A blizzard in Atlanta...impossible.

And suddenly more of Luke's words came back to her, after she'd claimed she wouldn't change her mind about attending the Valentine's party.

Maybe fate will intervene.

8

Carol stood mesmerized by the alien sight of snow falling in Atlanta until she realized that there would be no going home to snuggle up with a good, erotic book. She was stranded at the Mystic Touch office. And she had two choices: return to her office and massage more paperwork…or go to the Valentine's Day company party.

The low throbbing in her temples from the bump on the head she'd received this morning made the thought of scrutinizing spreadsheets unbearable.

The party seemed to be the lesser of the two evils.

So she trudged back to the elevator and rode

down to the basement, unwinding her scarf from her neck. She could hear the noise of the party even before the elevator stopped. When the doors opened, the full force of music, laughter and voices blasted her. Her stomach churned—she didn't want to be here, and she couldn't think of a single person who wanted her here.

She stepped off the elevator, feeling self-conscious in her winter coat, thinking she should've returned to her office and dropped her things there. Instead she stood there holding her briefcase awkwardly while everyone else held a glass of pink punch.

A few heads turned in her direction, but after a quick downturn of their mouths, they turned away. The blatant snub sliced through her, but she kept scanning, looking for a friendly face.

She landed on Luke. He caught sight of her and his expression turned from surprise to something else that accompanied a smile. He said something to the person he was talking to, then turned and walked in her direction.

It seemed silly now that she'd dug in her

heels about not attending the party. Heat rose in her cheeks as he stopped in front of her.

"Snow," he said with a grin. "What brings you back?"

"Snow," she said matter-of-factly.

"Huh?"

"It's snowing." She pointed to the ceiling. Since the basement had no windows, everyone else was oblivious to the outside conditions. "A blizzard, actually."

"So you're stranded." Then he made a rueful noise. "I'm sorry—you probably don't feel like being here. Tracy told me about the bump on the head. You should've told me that's why you didn't want to come to the party. I would've left you alone."

His concern left her flustered and her tongue suddenly didn't work.

"Let me take your coat," he offered, reaching to help her out of the heavy garment. "In fact, let's put your coat and briefcase in the storage room."

She followed him slowly, wondering if people were watching them as they disappeared down the hallway. Sadly, though, everyone seemed keen on ignoring her. He unlocked the door of the storage room, then he grabbed her hand and pulled her inside, allowing the door to close behind them.

Her pulse rocketed. "Luke, what are you doing?"

He flipped on the lights, then smiled at her. "Sorry. Overkill, I know, just to give you a Valentine's gift." He hung her coat on a hook, then reached high on a shelf and removed a heart-shaped box of chocolates. When he turned back to her, he looked sheepish.

"It's silly, I guess. I saw this and it reminded me of you."

Carol felt flush with pleasure—until she looked at the box. A large snowflake adorned the top. That was her—cold as ice…like an icicle. The card he'd slipped in her tote bag taunted her. "Very funny," she said, handing it back to him.

His eyebrows drew together. "What do you mean?"

Hurt barbed through her chest. "I get the whole frosty, cold-as-ice thing. I know what people say about me, that they call me Ice

Princess." She turned and reached for her coat. "This was a bad idea—I think I'll wait out the storm in my office."

His fingers encircled her wrist. "Hey."

She turned back and looked up at him.

"That's not how I think of you," he said, his brown eyes pensive. "I bought the candy because of the snowflake—get it...? Snow... flake?"

Carol wet her lips. She wanted to believe him...but why would Luke Chancellor buy her candy?

"Sorry if I overreacted," she said. "I'm sure you bought candy for other coworkers."

"No," he said, then pulled her closer. "Just you, Snow."

His mouth lowered toward hers. She expected him to pull back at the last second, but instead, suddenly, his warm lips were on hers. It was jolting, the sense of connection, like she was being plugged into a socket. His tongue swept against hers, sending shock waves of desire coursing through her limbs. It had been so long since she'd felt these sensations that everything seemed new...fresh. Her mind and body reeled from the raw power in Luke's probing kiss.

He lifted his head and looked into her eyes. "I've been wanting to do that for so long."

Her chest rose and fell as she struggled to fill her lungs. She couldn't form words. How could she tell him that he'd just tapped into a deep, still well...unleashed a cataclysmic reaction in her body...awakened a sleeping giant? He couldn't know the depths to which she'd buried her sexual soul...and how amazing it felt to have it resurrected.

He wiped his hand over his mouth. "If you're going to slap me, get it over with."

She lifted her hand, then curled it around his neck and pulled his lips down on hers, hard.

Luke moaned into her mouth and the vibration echoed through her body. He pulled her against him and their hands were frenzied, roaming over each other's bodies. He smoothed his palms down her back and pulled her sex against the hardened ridge of his erection. The physical proof of what they were about to do made Carol dizzy with lust. He picked her up by the waist and set her on a table, then slid up her skirt so she could spread her knees.

"Wait," she said, then nodded to the door. "What if someone knows how to get in?"

He left her long enough to wedge a straight-back chair under the doorknob, then returned to her with a vengeance, wedging himself between her thighs.

Carol's pumps fell off with succeeding thuds. She leaned back on her hands to brace herself, then squeezed his hips with her knees. Her breasts, her sex, her entire body throbbed with anticipation.

"Oh, no," he murmured suddenly, then put a hand to his head. "I don't have a condom. I'm sorry."

She winced, but pulled his mouth back to hers. "Then we'll have to be creative." She was taking a huge risk—she wasn't sexually experienced and James hadn't been particularly adventurous. She'd have to draw on what she'd learned between the pages of the erotic novels she'd read and hope that her enthusiasm would make up for her lack of expertise.

Luke's response was fierce, his tongue stabbing into her mouth, a silent promise to be creative for as long as necessary. He kissed his way down her neck, then plucked at the buttons on her white blouse until it lay open, exposing her lacy bra. Sighing into her skin, he laved the flesh above her bra, until she couldn't bear the suspense anymore and unhooked the front closure.

One breast fell into his hand, the other into his mouth. He licked her nipple, then pulled it into his mouth, leaving her shuddering with pleasure. But they were both too frantic to linger. Luke pushed her skirt to her waist, then rolled down her panty hose and underwear to open her sex to him. When he knelt and flicked his tongue against her folds, Carol dug her fingers into his shoulders. She couldn't think... couldn't speak...could only feel the amazing wonderfulness of having his mouth against her most intimate places. It was a first for her and the sensations pummeling her were almost overwhelming, leaving her languid and elastic.

He suckled the tiny sensitive nub that housed her orgasms, immediately coaxing one out of its hiding place to roam languorously as it made its way to the surface. Carol urged him on with moans and squeezes, riding on pure physical pleasure until the sensations in her womb began to swing with centrifugal force. The circles of liquid bliss grew tighter and heavier, swirling with growing intensity until her body bucked with a deep, intense climax.

Carol bit down on her own hand to muffle the sounds of her release, although the throbbing bass of the party music all but guaranteed that no one could hear them. Luke nuzzled her sex until she quieted, but she was eager to pleasure him, too. She pulled him to his feet, then loosened his belt and unzipped his pants to free his imposing erection.

When she clasped the rigid length of him, he gasped, his eyes hooded with desire. Carol slid from the table to kneel in front of him. She'd never done this before, but from what she'd read, it was hard to go wrong while performing oral sex on a man. She gingerly took his erection into her mouth, surprised by his silky hardness. He groaned with pleasure, his thighs tensing. She could sense his restraint as he allowed her to set the pace, using her tongue and taking cues from his sounds of gratification. She loved pleasing him orally, experimenting, making him feel the way he'd made her feel.

And she reasoned she must be doing it right when he whispered that he was about to come. He withdrew from her mouth and pulled her to her feet, holding her body against his while he stroked his erection. He kissed her neck and shoulder, then tensed and shuddered. She felt his contractions, then the wetness of his release on her stomach. He held her as his breathing slowed, then sighed into her ear.

"Wow," he murmured. "What just happened?"

Carol stiffened. Maybe it was the sound of his voice breaking the spell. Maybe it was the sensation of his seed cooling on her stomach. Maybe it was the realization that they were in a dusty storage room, with all their coworkers mere steps away, probably wondering what they were doing. The weight of remorse staggered her. What had she done?

Luke pulled back, then removed a handkerchief from his back pocket to mop up her stomach. "Go to dinner with me tomorrow night," he urged.

Her mind raced as she straightened her clothes. "Tomorrow…you mean Valentine's Day?"

"Yes."

She turned her back to retrieve her underwear and panty hose, stepping into them as quickly and modestly as she could manage in such a confining space. So Luke didn't mind dumping the "special lady" he already had plans with. So like a man. But she knew what it felt like to be on the other end of that equation…and since Luke had left a string of broken hearts in his wake, she'd be just another conquest. Good grief, for all she knew, this storage room might be his own private place to fool around.

Panic licked at her neck until she realized the situation played perfectly into her original plan to seduce him, then dump him. She turned back and forced a note of casual nonchalance into her voice. "I don't think so. Look, this was just a one-time thing to satisfy curiosity.

I'm not curious anymore." She adopted a blasé expression.

Luke pursed his mouth. "Uh…okay."

She slipped her feet into her pumps. "Why don't you go out first so it'll seem less suspicious if anyone is watching."

"Okay." He hesitated, then rechecked his clothing and made his way to the door.

She turned away and closed her eyes. That was close. Having sex with Luke Chancellor might not have been the smartest move, but thinking it meant something would be the biggest mistake.

"Carol."

She schooled her expression, then turned around. "Yes?"

"Whatever he did to you, I'm sorry."

She swallowed. "Who are you talking about?"

Luke shrugged. "I don't know. Whoever it was who hurt you so badly."

Her jaw loosened, but he didn't wait for a reply. He slipped out the door and it closed behind him.

She fisted her hands, shaken by his words…

and angered. If she wasn't interested in being swept into Luke's emotional riptide, then she must be damaged. His reaction only reinforced her decision not to have dinner with him, not to foster false hope that a sexual encounter, no matter how explosive, would lead to something more serious.

Carol patted her hair, then realized with some small measure of relief that her headache was gone. She lifted her hand to her forehead to find that the goose egg she'd been nursing was also gone. It was something to be grateful for on an otherwise lousy day.

From the floor, a glint of metal caught her eye—her silver-and-emerald earring. In all the commotion this morning, she'd neglected to take it with her. She knelt to retrieve it from under the shelf, but lost her balance and bumped the shelving unit accidentally. Above her, she heard a scraping noise, and when she looked up, something large was bearing down on her.

Despite the sense of déjà vu, Carol didn't have time to put up her hand. Pain exploded in her head, then everything went black again.

9

Someone was shaking Carol by the shoulder.

"Carol…Carol?"

The voice was familiar…but out of context. Carol opened her eyes to blink Gabrielle Pope's face into view, then winced at the pain that stabbed her temple.

"Oh, good—you're not dead," Gabrielle said.

"What are you doing here?" Carol asked.

"Just popping in to give you a hand."

"A hand with what?"

"Can you sit up?"

"I think so." Carol pushed up to a sitting position, then lifted her hand to her head, where a goose egg had formed—again. "Ow."

"That looks painful," Gabrielle said. "Maybe I should call an ambulance."

"No," Carol said, gingerly pushing to her feet. "It's just a bump on the head. I'll be fine. I need to get back to work."

"Not yet," Gabrielle said. "First I have to show you something."

"What?"

Gabrielle pointed to a boxy computer screen sitting on the floor nearby. "A memory of Valentine's Day Past."

Confused, Carol watched as the monitor blinked on, then zoomed in on a woman sitting at a restaurant table alone, as if she were waiting for someone.

Carol gasped. "That's me."

Gabrielle nodded.

It suddenly dawned on Carol what she was watching. "I don't want to see this," she said, turning her head away.

"But you must," Gabrielle said gently.

Carol reluctantly pivoted back to the monitor, dread billowing in her stomach. The woman sitting at the restaurant table looked younger…

hopeful…in love. Gabrielle leaned forward and turned a volume knob.

A handsome blond man walked up to the table and leaned down to place a kiss on the young woman's temple. "Hi, sweetheart."

Carol's heart squeezed. James…it had been so long since she'd heard his voice, she'd almost forgotten what it sounded like. Music to her heart.

"Happy Valentine's Day," he said, then slid a small gift box across the table.

Carol remembered how her pulse had skipped higher at the size of the box, thinking—hoping—it contained a ring. She had opened the box with shaking fingers, and although her heart had dropped in disappointment at the sight of silver-and-emerald earrings, she had pulled a bright smile out of thin air and gushed over the thoughtful present.

"Emeralds," he said, "are the sign of a successful love."

She put the earrings on and leaned forward to thank him with a kiss. After they ordered drinks, she slipped her gift for him out of her purse. "Happy Valentine's Day," she said, pushing it toward him.

Carol watched her younger self, her stomach taut with nerves.

James opened the box and seemed surprised. "A ring? I love it, darling." He removed the chunky horseshoe ring with small diamonds from its case and slipped it on his finger.

Carol was pleased that it looked classy, yet masculine on his hand.

"Thank you," he said, then leaned forward for another kiss.

She shifted nervously on her chair. "Actually, it's not just a ring."

James's eyebrows shot up. "Oh?"

"Actually...I was hoping...that is, I was wondering..."

"Yes? What is it, dear?"

"James...will you marry me?"

Watching the scene unfold, Carol emitted a mournful sound. She knew too well what was coming next.

James dropped his gaze, then took his time lifting his glass for a drink. Finally, he used his napkin to wipe the perspiration from his forehead. She noticed his pallor had gone gray.

"James?" Carol prompted. "Is something wrong?"

He reached across the table to clasp her hand. "No. I mean…yes. I've wanted to tell you something, but the timing never seemed right."

Carol remembered that at this point, her first worry had been that James was seriously ill. How naive she'd been.

"Whatever it is," she said, "tell me now."

"This isn't easy to say, but…I've been spending time with another woman, and…she's going to have my baby."

Carol watched her younger self, the myriad of emotions that played over her face—disbelief, shock, hurt, anger. She jerked her hand from his as if she'd been burned. "You're lying."

James drained his drink, then set the glass on the table with a thud. "I'm sorry, but I want to do the right thing. She and I are getting married. See you around." Then he got up and walked out of the frame.

Carol had always wondered what she must've looked like that night to other diners…sitting there dressed up, wearing the earrings James had just given her, her face a mask of incredulity. Now she knew. She looked as if she'd been punched in the stomach, or as if she expected James to come back and announce that he'd been playing a practical joke. In fact, she'd sat there and ordered and eaten a meal by herself, just in case James did return.

He hadn't, of course.

Carol's cheeks felt wet, and she realized she was crying. "Other than losing my parents, that was the worst night of my life."

"I know," Gabrielle said quietly. "And I'm sorry to make you relive it. But you need to see that you are not to blame for what James did. His irresponsible and hurtful behavior is his to own. You did nothing wrong."

"I trusted him," Carol said. "That was wrong."

"Trusting James was misguided," Gabrielle corrected, "but it wasn't wrong. It's never wrong to love. It's James's loss that he took advantage of your love instead of returning it."

But Carol's heart still squeezed at the injustice. James had led her on for years, gave her reason to believe they had a future together, all while having an affair and getting another woman pregnant. In hindsight, she wondered if he would've ever told her about the other woman if she hadn't proposed and forced the issue.

When the pain started to suffocate her, Carol turned away from the monitor. "I have to go."

"Very well," Gabrielle said. "But don't forget, it's never wrong to love."

Carol walked to the door of the supply room and let herself out in the hall, shaking her head at what she'd just experienced.

Dreamed, more like it. Walking back to the elevator, she reached up to touch the tender skin on her forehead. Maybe she'd taken a harder hit than she realized.

That would explain her hallucination.

As she approached the elevator, she realized preparations were already underway for the afternoon party.

Carol squinted. But the party had already happened...hadn't it?

Red decorations of cupids and hearts abounded. Blowups of some of the company's Valentine's Day cards leaned against the wall, including the "take no prisoners" card she'd seen on her assistant's desk. Cupid looked even more menacing at life-size.

Thankfully, she didn't see Luke among the volunteers.... She wasn't ready to face him after their encounter during the party.

She stopped and looked back to the party preparations, again disoriented. The workers threw her a look of distaste before turning back to their tasks. Well, even if other events were confused in her head, one thing remained true—everyone hated her for voting against giving the employee bonuses.

On the elevator ride up, Carol did some mental calculations to try to clear her head. She counted backward from one hundred by multiples of nine...she recited the presidents of the United States.

Everything seemed to be in working order.

When the doors opened and she walked into

her department, Tracy looked up from her desk where she was playing with her new computer. In fact, everyone was still preoccupied with the new equipment she and Luke had scavenged from the storage room.

"I understand Luke Chancellor was up all night installing these machines for us," Tracy said, her eyes dreamy. "When you see him, give him a big kiss for me, will you?"

Carol blinked. "Excuse me?"

"In the directors' meeting," Tracy said, then glanced at the clock. "You're going to be late."

Carol massaged her temples. "Um, Tracy… what day is it?"

Tracy narrowed her eyes. "Friday, February thirteenth. Are you okay, Ms. Snow?"

"Yes," Carol lied. In truth, a low, throbbing headache had settled into her crown. She stopped by the ladies' room to arrange her hair over the reddened bump on her forehead, then proceeded to the room where the directors' meeting was held. Before entering, she took a deep breath, then pushed open the door.

Her fellow directors looked up and she could

tell not all of them were relieved to see her. Luke Chancellor sat at the head of the table. It was the first time she'd seen him clothed since she'd seen him naked. She hoped it wouldn't be awkward.

He smiled up at her. "We were just getting ready to send out a search party for you, Carol."

She settled into an empty chair. "Sorry I'm late."

"We heard a Good Samaritan delivered new computer equipment to your department this morning," Janet, the art director, said with a smile.

All gazes slid toward Luke. He held up his hands. "It was Carol's idea—I just... facilitated."

She set her jaw—how did he do that? Manage to sound humble and still take credit?

And why wasn't he acknowledging—in private glances, at least—that they'd recently shared some very good oral sex?

"We were about to take another vote on the issue of bonuses," Luke said, all business. "I think it's pretty clear that anyone dissenting is following your lead, Carol, so I guess we can cut to the chase by asking if you've changed your mind on paying out a one-time bonus?"

The weight of a roomful of stares shifted to her. Carol glanced from side to side to see if anyone else remembered having this exact meeting at…sometime.

Luke looked hopeful, and Carol knew he was thinking of her previous comment that she might reconsider her position. But that was before he'd turned all her employees against her. Before he'd given her a blinding orgasm in the storage room and made her feel again. This might be her one and only chance…again…to put Luke Chancellor in his place.

"No, I haven't changed my mind," she said carefully, feeling strangely like a doppel-gänger.

Disappointment colored Luke's face. His mouth flattened, then he shrugged. "I guess that's that."

Carol clapped her hands. "Good. If that's all, I need to get back to work. The party means I have only four hours to get done what I'd normally do in eight." Then she stopped. "There is a party today, right?"

"Right," Luke said, his mouth tight. "And yes, that's all."

Carol's gaze roved over him, recalling the size of his erection, and the sounds the man made when he climaxed.

Or had she dreamed the encounter as well?

"Something else on your mind?" Luke asked.

That little swirly trick you do with your tongue. "Uh…no." She pushed to her feet and left. On the way back to her office, Carol massaged her temples, trying to alleviate the headache that had yet to ease. When she reached her department, she walked the gauntlet of angry stares from her employees and closed her office door. There she downed some aspirin and waited for the feeling of vindication to descend. She'd proved to Luke that her opinion still meant something around here…that there was at least one woman he couldn't charm into submission.

She squinted. But if she'd given him a

blowjob, didn't that mean she'd already sub-mitted?

Regardless, sitting here in the wake of her power, the victory of winning the vote felt strangely hollow. She gave herself a mental shake, reasoning that she could hardly feel good about anything while nursing a headache. She would savor the success later, in private.

When she was alone. Completely, abso-lutely, utterly alone.

She stopped, certain she'd had that thought before—déjà vu?

Carol pushed a button on the intercom and told Tracy she wasn't to be disturbed, then spent the morning plowing through a mountain of paperwork that seemed amazingly simple, as if she'd done it before and already knew all the answers.

But since her headache wasn't letting up, she decided she'd skip the Valentine's Day party and just go home, maybe tuck in with a good book, something she could suggest as a selec-tion for the Red Tote Book Club.

While she was thinking about it, she pulled

out her phone and sent Gabrielle an update via text message.

Seduction achieved. Details later.

A couple of minutes later, Gabrielle replied.

Surrender to love, Carol.

Carol frowned at the message. Love? Who said anything about love?

And *surrender?* Never.

A knock sounded at her door, then it creaked open.

"Tracy, I asked not to be disturbed," Carol said without looking up.

"Don't get mad at her," Luke said.

Carol lifted her head to see the man of the hour standing in the threshold. He gestured behind him. "Tracy said you didn't want to be disturbed, but I told her I'd take full responsibility for defying your orders."

He looked just as handsome in brown slacks and pale blue dress shirt, minus a tie, as he had…before. Carol's pulse quickened, but she reminded herself that he wasn't to be trusted. Along with her memory, apparently.

"What do you want, Chancellor?"

"I thought it would be nice if we walked into the party together, a show of solidarity."

She stood and began packing her briefcase. "I'm not going to the party."

He gave a little laugh. "Why not?"

"Because I'd rather go home, that's why."

"Go home to what?" he asked. "A book?"

At his mocking tone, Carol bit down on the inside of her cheek. "What's it to you?" She looked up and her anger surged to the surface. "I mean, really, Luke, as if you care."

He blinked and visibly pulled back. "That's the thing—I *do* care... Although I'm starting to wonder why."

She rolled her eyes—it was a preposterous statement considering the fact that he'd compared her to an icicle that wouldn't thaw. "Save it, Chancellor. Go." She made a shooing motion. "Go be the life of the party, the sales hero, the company playboy."

Once again she'd spoken with more venom than she'd intended, but after the words were out...well, she couldn't take them back...she didn't think...

"Exactly what did I do to make you so angry?" Luke asked.

"Well, for starters, you told everyone I was the reason no one is getting a bonus."

"I didn't tell everyone," he said. "In fact, I didn't tell *any*one. There were eight other directors in that meeting. But, when it comes down to it, *aren't* you the reason no one is getting a bonus?"

Carol slammed her briefcase shut. "I voted no because I think there are better things to do with the company money."

"I know—you said your department needed new equipment, and I helped you get it. And you still voted no."

"That's the other thing. All my employees think you're a hero."

"And that's a bad thing?"

"At my expense."

He gave a little laugh. "Why didn't you tell them that you helped me? You were the one with the wish list, the one who knew what kind of equipment everyone had and what they needed."

She shrugged. "I…I guess I didn't want to feel like I had to toot my own horn."

"I give up." He shook his head and started toward the door. With his hand on the doorknob, he looked back. "I hope you change your mind about coming to the party."

She walked over to her coatrack and shrugged into her coat. "I won't."

"Then maybe fate will intervene." He smiled, then strode out.

Then Carol remembered—the blizzard! Maybe she could get out in front of it. She gathered her things and dashed out of her office. Only Tracy remained in the department, sitting at her desk obediently, although she glanced longingly at the clock.

"I'm leaving," Carol announced as she dashed by. "Here's the memo you need to redo." She tossed the piece of paper in the direction of her assistant's desk.

"You're not staying for the party?"

"No!"

"Be careful driving home," Tracy called behind her. "I hear a winter storm is blowing in!"

Carol sprinted through empty departments toward the elevator. Everyone was already in the basement for the party. As she waited for the elevator, something in particular that Luke said came floating back to her.

That's the thing—I do care...

Carol shook her head. She didn't want him to care. She didn't need the complication of a man in her life who cared. Because even if he cared now, at this precise moment, it would be short-lived.

Frustrated that the elevator was taking so long, she opted for the stairs and took them as quickly as her high-heeled pumps would allow. She burst out of the stairwell into an empty lobby. When she turned toward the front entrance, a rumble sounded overhead. She knew that sound. Sure enough, a bulging purple sky burst open, sending enormous snowflakes to the ground, where they were swept up into a cyclonic wind. Within seconds, the outdoors was enveloped in a thick, impermeable blur of white.

Another blizzard in Atlanta...impossible.

Fate had once again intervened.

_10_

Carol stood mesmerized by the alien sight of snow falling in Atlanta until she realized that there would be no going home to snuggle up with a good, erotic book. She was stranded at the Mystic Touch office. And she had two choices: return to her office and massage more paperwork…or go to the Valentine's Day company party.

The low throbbing in her temples from the bump on the head she'd received this morning made the thought of scrutinizing spreadsheets unbearable.

The party seemed to be the lesser of the two evils…if she could resist Luke.

She trudged back to the elevator and rode

down to the basement, unwinding her scarf from her neck. She could hear the noise of the party even before the elevator stopped. When the doors opened, the full force of music, laughter and voices blasted her. Her stomach churned—she didn't want to be here, and she couldn't think of a single person who wanted her here.

She stepped off the elevator, feeling self-conscious in her winter coat, thinking once again that she should've returned to her office and dropped her things there. Instead she stood there holding her briefcase awkwardly while everyone else held a glass of pink punch.

A few heads turned in her direction, but after a quick downturn of their mouths, they turned away. The blatant snub cut deep, but she kept scanning, looking for a friendly face.

She landed on Luke. He caught sight of her and his expression turned from surprise to something else that accompanied a smile. He said something to the person he was talking to, then turned and walked in her direction.

But he was not looking at her like a man

who had intimate knowledge of her choice in underwear.

"Snow," he said with a grin. "What brings you back?"

"Snow," she said matter-of-factly.

"Huh?"

"It's snowing." She pointed to the ceiling. Since the basement had no windows, everyone else was oblivious to the outside conditions. "A blizzard, actually."

"So you're stranded. Let me take your coat," he offered, reaching to help her out of the heavy garment. "In fact, let's put your coat and brief-case in the storage room."

"Um…that's okay…I'll just hang on to them."

"Are you sure? Come with me anyway—I have something to give you."

The box of candy. And she really didn't want their coworkers to see him giving her candy. Carol followed him slowly down the hall, dismayed that her body was already loosening for him, warming, softening. Desire struck her low and hard.

He unlocked the door of the storage room,

held it open for her, then allowed it to close behind them.

"You've piqued my curiosity," she offered.

"It's not much," he said, reaching high on a shelf to remove a heart-shaped box of chocolates.

She realized if she didn't act hurt over the whole snowflake/cold as ice/Ice Princess connotation of the blue snowflake box, then he wouldn't feel compelled to tell her that wasn't how he thought of her, which would lead to her saying he probably bought candy for other coworkers, which would lead to him saying no, only for her, which would lead to the kiss that had been her undoing.

When he turned back to her, he looked sheepish. "It's silly, I guess. I saw this and it reminded me of you."

She opened her mouth to saw how much she liked the blue snowflake box, but stopped when she saw instead a pink satin box that read "Kiss Me."

"Kiss me?" she squeaked.

He scratched his head. "To be honest, I'm

not quite sure why I bought that one. It just seemed...right."

When his mouth lowered toward hers, she knew she should stop him. Instead, she met his warm lips, rejoicing in the familiar feel of his kiss...the connection...the shock waves. It had been so long since she'd felt these sensations... an entire twenty-four hours ago, at this same point in time. Her mind and body reeled from the raw power in Luke's probing kiss.

He lifted his head and looked into her eyes. "Why do I have the feeling we've done this before?"

"Kismet," she whispered, then curled her hand around his neck and pulled his lips down on hers, hard.

Luke moaned into her mouth and the vibration echoed through her body. He pulled her against him and their hands became frenzied, roaming over each other's bodies. He smoothed his palms down her back, over her buttocks, and pulled her sex against the hardened ridge of his erection. The physical proof of what they were about to do...again...made Carol dizzy with lust.

He stopped, his gaze bouncing around the room, looking for a suitable surface.

Carol pointed to the nearby table. "Take me there."

He picked her up by the waist and set her on the table, then slid up her skirt so she could spread her knees.

"Wait," she said, then nodded to the door. "Can you wedge a chair under the doorknob?"

He did, then came back to stand between her thighs.

Carol's pumps fell off with succeeding thuds. She leaned back on her hands to brace herself, then squeezed his hips with her knees. Her breasts, her sex, her entire body throbbed with anticipation, especially since now she knew what to expect.

"Oh, no," he murmured suddenly, then put a hand to his head. "I don't have a condom. I'm sorry."

Her shoulders fell—damn, she'd forgotten that part.

She pulled his mouth back to hers. "Then we'll have to be creative." There were still lots of things from the pages of the erotic novels she'd read for the Red Tote Book Club that she wanted to try.

Luke's response was fierce, his tongue stabbing into her mouth, a silent promise to be creative for as long as necessary. He kissed his way down her neck, then plucked at the buttons on her white blouse until it lay open, exposing her lacy bra. Impatient to have his mouth on her, she unhooked the front closure.

One breast fell into his hand, the other into his mouth. He licked her nipple, then pulled it into his mouth, leaving her shuddering with pleasure. But they were both too frantic to linger. Luke pushed her skirt to her waist, then rolled down her panty hose and underwear to expose her sex to him. When he knelt and flicked his tongue against her folds, Carol's toes curled. She couldn't think…couldn't speak…could only feel the amazing wonderfulness of having his mouth against her most intimate places. It felt like the first time all over again. The sensations pummeling her were almost overwhelming, leaving her languid and elastic.

He suckled the tiny sensitive nub that housed her orgasms, instantly coaxing one from its hiding place. But instead of roaming languorously as it made its way to the surface, this one zoomed for air. The speed and intensity took her and Luke both by surprise. Carol bucked against his mouth to ride out a deep, powerful climax.

Carol bit down on her own hand to muffle the sounds of her release, although the throbbing bass of the party music all but guaranteed that no one could hear them. Luke nuzzled her sex until she quieted, but she was eager to pleasure him, too. She pulled him to his feet, then loosened his belt and unzipped his pants to free his imposing erection.

When she clasped the rigid length of him, he gasped, his eyes hooded with desire. Carol slid from the table to kneel in front of him, then took his erection into her mouth as far as she could, reveling in his silky hardness. He groaned with pleasure, his thighs tensing. This time pleasing him orally felt more natural, less awkward. She experimented with nuances in pressure and texture to see how he responded.

And this time when he whispered he was about to come, instead of allowing him to withdraw, she clasped his hips and pulled him deeper into her mouth. When he realized her intention, she sensed his added excitement. Within a few seconds, he tensed and shuddered. She felt his contractions, then the spurt of his release in her mouth.

At length his breathing slowed. He pulled her to her feet and kissed her soundly. "Wow," he murmured. "What just happened?"

Carol steeled herself, but was dismayed when a familiar sense of remorse started to close in. Which only made sense, really. She'd known she and Luke were going to have an empty encounter, and yet she'd gone along with it…again…as if something was going to be different this time around.

But it wasn't.

Luke pulled back. "Go to dinner with me tomorrow night."

Carol straightened her clothes. "Tomorrow… you mean Valentine's Day?"

"Yes."

She turned her back to retrieve her underwear and panty hose, stepping into them as quickly and modestly as she could manage in such a confining space. Once again, Luke didn't mind dumping the "special lady" he already had plans with. Carol knew she should be flattered, but instead all she could think about was the woman who'd been looking forward to a romantic evening relegated to sitting at home. Playing the home version of *Wheel of Fortune* while she watched the show on TV.

Not that she'd ever done that herself.

And this time next year, Luke would have moved on to yet another woman, and she'd be the one dodging him on the elevator or perhaps looking for a new job after a bad breakup.

She turned back and forced a note of casual nonchalance into her voice. "I don't think so. Look, this was just a two-time thing to satisfy… curiosity."

He squinted. "Two times?"

"I mean one-time," she said quickly. "A *one*-time thing to satisfy curiosity. And I'm not curious anymore." She adopted a blasé expression.

Luke pursed his mouth. "Uh…okay."

She slipped her feet into her pumps. "Why don't you leave first so it'll seem less suspicious if anyone is watching."

"Okay." He hesitated, then rechecked his clothing and made his way to the door.

She turned away and closed her eyes. That was close. Having sex with Luke Chancellor… twice…might not have been the smartest move, but thinking it meant something different this time around would be the biggest mistake ever.

"Carol."

She schooled her expression, then turned around. "Yes?"

Luke's expression was pensive. "I have a feeling there's something here between us, but for some reason, you're holding back. But I also have a feeling that this is totally out of my hands."

He didn't wait for a reply. He slipped out the door and it closed behind him.

She fisted her hands, frustrated by a situation

that was growing increasingly complicated. How was she supposed to make any decisions when the present double-backed onto the past?

Carol checked her clothing and smoothed her hair, realizing with some small measure of relief that her headache was gone. She lifted her hand to her forehead to find that the goose egg she'd been nursing was also gone. It was something to be grateful for on an otherwise lousy day.

From the floor, a glint of metal caught her eye—her silver-and-emerald earring. She still hadn't managed to get out of here with it. She bent over from the waist to retrieve the earring from under the shelf, keeping her feet firmly planted so as not to lose her balance. She grasped the earring, but when she straightened, she bumped the shelving unit accidentally. Above her, she heard a scraping noise, and when she looked up, something large was bearing down on her.

Despite the overwhelming sense of déjà vu,

Carol didn't have time to put up her hand. Pain exploded in her head, then everything went black *again*.

11

Someone was shaking Carol by the shoulder.

"Carol…wake up. Carol?"

Gabrielle Pope was back. Carol opened her eyes, and winced at the obligatory pain in her head. "You again?"

Gabrielle nodded. "I'm afraid so."

"Why are you involved in my hallucinations?"

"You have to ask yourself that."

Carol pressed her lips together. She'd have to give it some thought…when she was actually conscious.

"Can you sit up?"

"Unless this bump on the head was worse than the last one." Carol pushed up to a sitting position, then lifted her hand to her head, where a goose egg had formed. "At least it's on the other side."

"Hm," Gabrielle said. "The fact that the bump is on the other side might mean something."

"What?"

"I have no idea…but you probably do."

"Don't confuse the unconscious girl," Carol said. "Why is this even happening to me?"

"Good question. Some people who suffer an emotional setback bury the memory instead of dealing with it. Once it begins to affect a person's present behavior and relationships, they might choose to see a therapist."

"Or join a book club," Carol offered.

"Yes. But the mind can only deal with so much stress before it has to find a release valve."

"Ergo these little blackouts?"

"Maybe," Gabrielle agreed. "If a person is afraid to process a memory, recalling that memory in a dream or under hypnosis is much safer."

"Like my memory of how James dumped me."

"Right. Similarly, if a person is afraid to try something new, visualization, dreams and hallucinations are a safe way to explore new experiences."

"Like a possible relationship with Luke?"

"Yes."

"What do you have for me today?" Carol asked, gesturing to the monitor lying in the floor on its side.

"A look at Valentine's Day Present—tomorrow, in fact."

Carol watched as the monitor blinked on, then zoomed in on a man stopping at a florist to get a dozen roses.

"That's Luke," Carol said.

On screen, he was knuckle-biting handsome in a dark suit and a light-colored shirt, with a tie.

"Considering how much he hates ties, he must be excited about his date," she offered.

"Wait and see," Gabrielle said.

Carol's heart thudded in her chest…would

she be Luke's date? If not, why would Gabrielle
be showing her the vision?

Luke walked out with a dozen white roses.

"Nice," Carol agreed. White would've been
her choice, too.

The next scene showed Luke driving up to
a restaurant and handing his keys to a valet.

"He's at Richardson's," Carol said happily.
"That's my favorite restaurant."

Luke got out of the car and walked around to
the passenger side to open the door. A woman's
legs appeared, then she alighted with Luke's
assistance and smiled up at him.

"That's not me," Carol said of the gorgeous,
busty blonde.

"I noticed," Gabrielle said drily.

"I don't recognize her, so she's not from the
office."

"Let's see," Gabrielle said, turning up the
volume.

Luke and the blonde chatted as they entered
the restaurant.

"I guess it was my lucky day when I decided
to go with my friend to the Steeplechase," the

woman gushed. "I never dreamed I'd meet someone like you, Luke."

She leaned in for a kiss and Luke obliged. He seemed attentive, but Carol noticed he had the same look in his eyes as when he was bored in a staff meeting. Still, the blonde looked as if she would be able to keep him entertained after they got past the niceties. A stab of jealousy caught Carol off guard…and she didn't like the feeling. One of the reasons she hadn't dated after James was because she didn't want to be a suspicious, jealous shrew, to make the new man in her life pay for the sins of her ex.

The scene faded and Carol thought they were finished, but then another scene opened onto the interior of a house, and zoomed in on a woman sitting tucked into a corner of a couch, wearing flannel pajamas.

"That's me," Carol said, making a face. Did those pajamas really look so old and ratty?

"Yes," Gabrielle said to her unasked question.

Carol frowned, then looked back to the monitor. She was holding a big bowl of popcorn in her lap. On the table next to her sat a two-liter bottle of diet soda with a giant straw. And next to the soda was the home edition of *Wheel of Fortune*. When the frame pulled back, the show *Wheel of Fortune* was also playing on the television.

Carol's cheeks burned. "It's an educational show," she murmured. Then she looked up. "I get the point."

"I hope so," Gabrielle said. "Because it's time for you to go."

"I know," Carol said, pointing to her suit— the one she'd put on Friday morning and the one she felt as if she'd lived in for a week. "I have a meeting." She stood, righted her clothes, and tossed a few extra things into her briefcase, just in case. Then she walked to the door of the storage room and let herself out in the hall, now more confused than ever. Gabrielle had tried to convince her that her hallucinations had some kind of meaning…but what if they were just a jumble of stored memories and random thoughts?

As she approached the elevator, she noticed that once again, preparations were underway for the afternoon party.

Carol winced. Not again.

Red decorations of cupids and hearts abounded. Blowups of some of the company's Valentine's Day cards leaned against the wall, including the "take no prisoners" card she'd seen on her assistant's desk. Cupid was still just as menacing at life-size.

Your best strategy is to surrender.

The volunteers exchanged eye rolls when she walked by. Apparently everyone still hated her. It was, it seemed, the one thing she could count on.

On the elevator ride up to her floor, Carol lifted one hand in a fist then the other, to make sure they matched, then she stood on one foot at a time.

"Are you okay?"

Mortified, Carol realized she'd performed the exercises in front of an elevator full of her coworkers.

"Fine," she murmured, but secretly wondered if she'd had some kind of stroke—neurological damage would explain the things she'd been experiencing.

When the doors opened and she walked into

her department, Tracy looked up from her desk
where she was playing with her "new" computer. All around the bullpen, employees were
comparing their machines and the peripheral
equipment she and Luke had scavenged from
the storage room.

"Word is that Luke Chancellor paid for
this equipment out of his own pocket," Tracy
declared.

Carol frowned. "What did I tell you about
watercooler rumors?"

Tracy blanched, then tapped her watch. "The
directors' meeting...you should get going."

Carol massaged her aching temples. "Um,
Tracy...just checking—what day is it?"

Tracy narrowed her eyes. "Friday, February
thirteenth. Are you okay, Ms. Snow?"

"Yes," Carol lied. She was actually getting used to the headache. She stopped by the
ladies' room to arrange her hair to cover the
angry bump on her forehead, then proceeded
to the room where the directors' meeting was
held. Being the bad guy was getting easier.

Her fellow directors looked up and once
again, she sensed not all of them were relieved

to see her. Luke Chancellor sat at the head of the table. Remembering how intimate they'd been only…a while ago…she was unable to keep the secret little smile off her face.

Luke shifted nervously in his chair. "We were just getting ready to send out a search party for you, Carol."

She settled into an empty chair. "Sorry I'm late."

"We heard a Good Samaritan delivered new computer equipment to your department this morning," Janet, the art director, said with a smile.

All gazes slid toward Luke. He held up his hands. "It was Carol's idea—I just… facilitated."

He flashed her a grin. She countered with a knowing smirk, which seemed to throw him off-balance.

"Uh…we were about to take another vote on the issue of bonuses," Luke said. "I think it's pretty clear that anyone dissenting is following your lead, Carol, so I guess we can cut to the chase by asking if you've changed your mind on paying out a one-time bonus?"

The weight of a roomful of stares shifted to her. Luke looked hopeful, and Carol knew he was thinking of her previous comment that she might reconsider her position. He seemed to have no knowledge of the positions she had already assumed for him, and vice versa. Carol studied her nails, enjoying the suspense.

"No, I haven't changed my mind," she finally announced.

Disappointment lined Luke's face. Carol watched him—was it her imagination or did he seem to take the news worse today than… before?

His mouth flattened, then he shrugged. "I guess that's that."

Carol clapped her hands. "Good. If that's all, I need to get back to work. The party means I have to squeeze eight hours of work into a four-hour day." She glanced at Luke. "There is a party today, right?"

"Right," Luke said, pulling a hand down his face. "And yes, that's all."

Carol felt a pang of concern for him, and stopped short of reaching over to touch his arm. "You okay, Chancellor?"

"Yeah, sure," he said. "I'm just exhausted today for some reason."

She smothered a smile with her hand. "Maybe you're coming down with something."

He nodded. "Yeah…maybe. I don't feel like myself."

"Funny—you feel like yourself to me."

He looked up. "Hm?"

Carol smiled. "Never mind. Hope you feel better." She pushed to her feet and left.

On the way back to her office, her mind swirled. Nothing that had happened today— over and over again—made sense.

What worried her most was that her mind was in some kind of endless loop triggered by trauma, and that her poor body lay in a coma in a hospital bed somewhere, withering away.

Would she be stuck reliving Friday, February the thirteenth forever?

When Carol reached her department, she once again braved the gauntlet of resentment from her employees and closed her office door. There she downed aspirin and waited for the feeling of vindication to finally descend. She'd commanded respect in the directors' meeting this morning in a way she'd never done before. She'd proved to Luke that her opinion still meant something around here…that there was at least one woman he couldn't charm into submission.

She squinted. Okay, strike that, since she'd already submitted to him twice.

Although, did submission count if he couldn't remember it?

Regardless, the victory of winning the vote this morning felt strangely empty. It seemed as if the more times she was able to wield her power, the less appealing it became.

Carol pushed a button on the intercom and told Tracy she wasn't to be disturbed, then spent the first half of the morning zipping through the mountain of paperwork on her desk that now seemed rote. She intended to leave early today—*before* the blizzard hit. Maybe if she could break the cycle of the sequence of events, things would get back to normal.

Midmorning, she began packing up her briefcase, but paused at a timid knock on the door.

"Yes?"

Tracy stuck her head inside. "I'm sorry, Ms. Snow, I know you don't want to be bothered, but I was hoping you'd be willing to help me with this memo that I can't seem to get right."

Frustration spike in Carol's chest, but at the pleading look on her assistant's face, she caved. "Sure, Tracy, let's have a cup of coffee and I'll answer whatever questions you have."

The sheer relief and happiness on the redhead's face was worth living another day within a day.

As expected, by the time she'd gone through the memo line by line to explain what she expected, it was almost time for the snow squall to descend. Outside the sky was bruised and bloated, the wind picking up exponentially.

While she had a free minute, she pulled out her phone and sent Gabrielle an update via text message.

Here we go again.

A couple of minutes later, Gabrielle replied.

Surrender to love, Carol.

Carol frowned at the message. Another repeat.

A knock sounded at her door.

"Come on in, Chancellor."

The door creaked open and he stuck his head in, his expression quizzical. "How did you know it was me?"

"Uh…I guessed," she said. "What can I do for you?"

She crossed her arms, and surveyed his brown slacks and pale blue dress shirt—minus a tie—thinking he had no idea the things they'd already done for each other.

"I thought it would be nice if we walked into the party together, a show of solidarity."

She worked her mouth back and forth. "Okay."

He blinked. "Okay?"

"Oh, now that I've agreed, you're going to change your mind?"

"Not at all. I guess I'm just surprised, that's all. You haven't exactly hidden your disdain for me and my ideas."

She sighed. "Look, the vote on the bonuses wasn't personal."

"I think it was. I think if any other director had proposed bonuses, you would've at least kept an open mind."

"And if any other director had voted against you, you wouldn't have tried to bribe them with refurbished equipment for her employees."

He pursed his mouth. "Touché. Are you ready to walk down?"

She glanced out the window to see the plum-colored clouds rolling in right on schedule. "Sure."

She picked up her briefcase and coat.

"Don't you want to leave those here?" he asked.

"I'll think I'll keep them close by," she said.

When they exited Carol's office, Tracy was the only employee in the area. The young woman was using the dissected memo as an example as she typed a new one on her laptop. Carol hoped she and her assistant were finally making headway toward a good working relationship.

As she and Luke walked toward the elevator, he jammed his fingers into his hair. "Is it just me, or does this seem like the longest day ever?"

"No," Carol said as she leaned against the elevator wall, "it's not just you."

12

The elevator stopped on the lobby level even though only Carol and Luke were on board and neither of them had pressed the lobby button. When the door opened, Luke stepped forward to press the Close Door button then stopped, staring out the window. "You're not going to believe this—it's a blizzard out there."

She smiled and nodded, not even bothering to look. "Uh-huh."

He stared at her. "But...it *never* snows in Atlanta."

"So they say," she agreed, then pushed the close door button.

She could hear the noise of the party even before the elevator stopped. When the doors opened, the full force of music, laughter and voices blasted her. Her stomach churned, both at the known and the unknown.

A few heads turned in her direction, but after a quick downturn of their mouths, they turned away.

"Ignore them," Luke said. "Hey, why don't we take your coat and briefcase to the storage room? I have something for you."

The candy. Which was connected to the kiss bone. Which was connected to the bone...bone. Carol followed him slowly down the hallway, fighting a groan that somehow turned into a moan.

He looked back at her. "Did you say something?"

"No."

He unlocked the door of the storage room, held it open for her, then allowed it to close behind them while he turned on lights.

"It's not much," he said, reaching high on a shelf to remove a heart-shaped box of chocolates.

"Did you say you feel a cold coming on?"

she asked in a desperate attempt to ward off the impending kiss of spiraling lust.

Luke shook his head. "No. Just a little tired for no reason I can put my finger on."

When he handed her the box of candy, his cheeks were tinged pink. "It's silly, I guess."

She opened her mouth to say that, in fact, *she* was feeling under the weather and wouldn't want to spread anything to him through a kiss, but stopped when she saw instead a red silk box that read "Be Mine." Surprise sparkled in her chest at the romantic nature of the gift.

Luke scratched his head. "To be honest, I'm not quite sure why I bought that one. It just seemed…right." He thumped his chest as if trying to self-administer CPR. "Lately I've been having these…fantasies…um, feelings…"

Apparently deciding actions spoke louder than words, he lowered his mouth toward hers. In the wake of his incredibly romantic gesture, Carol's bogus contagion defense went out the window. She lifted her mouth to accept his kiss, knowing what his warm lips would feel like before they even made contact with hers. She sighed through the overlapping of sensations that were both new and familiar. Far removed from their first kiss, her mind and body still reeled from the raw power in Luke's probing tongue.

He lifted his head and looked into her eyes. "Do you believe in déjà vu?"

"Yes," she whispered, then curled her hand around his neck and pulled his lips down on hers, hard.

Luke moaned into her mouth and the vibration echoed through her body. He pulled her against him and their hands became frenzied, roaming over each other's bodies. He smoothed his palms down her back, over her buttocks, and pulled her sex against the hardened ridge of his erection. The physical proof of what they were about to do...yet again...made Carol dizzy with lust.

He stopped, his gaze bouncing around the room, looking for a suitable surface.

Carol pointed to the nearby table. "Take me there."

He picked her up by the waist and set her on the table, then slid up her skirt so she could spread her knees.

"Wait," she said, then nodded to the door. "Can you wedge a chair under the doorknob?"

"Good thinking," he said. After the chair was in place, he came back to stand between her thighs.

Carol's pumps fell off with succeeding thuds. She leaned back on her hands to brace herself, then squeezed his hips with her knees. Her breasts, her sex, her entire body throbbed with anticipation, especially since now she knew what to expect.

"Oh, no," he murmured suddenly, then put a hand to his head. "I don't have a condom. I'm sorry."

"There's one in my briefcase," she said, pointing. "Top compartment."

She was learning.

There were, after all, lots of things from the pages of the erotic novels she'd read for the Red Tote Book Club she wanted to try that required full contact.

Luke was back with the condom in record time, grinning. "I'm impressed, Snow. And grateful." He kissed his way down her neck, then plucked at the buttons on her white blouse until it lay open, exposing her naked breasts.

This morning she'd skipped the bra entirely.

He cupped one breast in his hand, and suckled the other one, pulling her nipple into his mouth until she shuddered with pleasure. But they were both too frantic to linger. Luke pushed her skirt to her waist, then rolled down her panty hose and underwear to expose her sex.

She loosened his belt and unzipped his pants to free his imposing erection. When she clasped the rigid length of him, he gasped, his eyes hooded with desire. She helped him roll on the condom and position his sheathed cock at her slick entrance.

"Now," she whispered in his ear.

He thrust forward, filling her completely. Carol wrapped her legs around his waist. She couldn't think...couldn't speak...could only feel the amazing wonderfulness of having his body melded with hers. It felt like the first time all over again. The sensations pummeling her were almost overwhelming, leaving her languid and elastic.

He massaged the tiny sensitive nub that housed her orgasms, looking into her eyes. "Snow, you're so sexy," he murmured, not bothering to hide his surprise. "I'm not going to last long."

His sex talk left her quivering and on the verge of a massive orgasm. He used his thumb to send her over the edge. Carol rode him through a deep, powerful climax, contracting around him. Before she had quieted, he shuddered his own release, groaning against her neck. The throbbing bass of the party music all but guaranteed that no one could hear them.

At length their breathing slowed. He pulled away, then kissed her thoroughly. "Wow," he murmured. "What just happened?"

Carol steeled herself, but felt the dreaded sense of remorse start to nibble away at the pure bliss she'd felt only seconds ago. Part of her felt manipulative, because she'd known what was going to happen, had even prepared for it. Luke, on the other hand, had no idea what was going on, only knew that he was conflicted about her. If he felt the ghost of their intimate encounters, he probably had the sense that his body knew her better than his brain actually did.

It had to be mystifying.

Luke pulled back. "Will you go to dinner with me tomorrow night?"

Carol straightened her clothes. "Tomorrow... you mean Valentine's Day?"

"Yes."

She turned her back to retrieve her underwear and panty hose, stepping into them as quickly and modestly as she could manage in such a confining space. "I thought you already had plans," she chided. "I heard you tell someone that you were having dinner with a 'special lady.'"

He grinned. "I will if you say yes. I haven't made any plans—that's my generic response."

Carol wet her lips, wavering. She wanted to say yes, wanted to go on a bona fide date with Luke, but she was already so...*attached* to him, she was terrified their relationship was already lopsided…and once again she'd be left out in the cold.

The scene of Valentine's Day Present that Gabrielle had played for her had shown Luke with the gorgeous blonde, meaning if Carol said no, he would meet the other woman and think enough of her to ask her to dinner instead.

So despite the great sex—most of which he was unaware of—and his heartfelt invitation, how much could Luke really care about her? She'd suffered enough humiliation in her relationship with James to last a lifetime.

It just wasn't worth the risk.

Carol turned back and forced a note of casual nonchalance into her voice. "I don't think so. Look, this was just a hookup to satisfy curiosity. And I'm not curious anymore." She adopted a blasé expression.

Luke's head went back, as if he'd been slapped. "Uh…okay."

She slipped her feet into her pumps. "Why don't you leave first so it'll seem less suspicious if anyone is watching."

"Okay." He hesitated, then rechecked his clothing and made his way to the door.

She turned away and closed her eyes. That was too close. Having sex with Luke Chancellor three times might not have been the smartest move, but thinking it meant something emotional this time around would be the biggest mistake ever.

"Luke," she said.

He turned back. "Yes?"

"Thank you for the candy."

He looked as if he wanted to say something, but thought better of it. Instead, he slipped out the door and it closed behind him.

Carol held her breath against the sudden pain squeezing her chest. She had the distinct feeling that her chance to be with Luke had just expired...in every alternate universe.

Wondering how she would get through the rest of the party, Carol checked her clothing and smoothed her hair, realizing with some small measure of relief that at least her headache was gone. She lifted her hand to her forehead to find the goose egg she'd been nursing was also gone. It was something to be grateful for in what seemed like an unending day.

From the floor, a glint of metal caught her

eye—her silver-and-emerald earring. She bit her lip. Was it worth one more try to retrieve the stray bauble that James had said was supposed to symbolize "a successful love"?

Carol looked around the room and smiled when she spied a heavy-duty industrial push broom. No more falling monitors.

She retrieved the broom, then used it to snag the earring and pull it out a safe distance from under the shelf where she could get to it without bumping into anything.

She leaned the broom against the shelving unit, then crouched to pick up the earring. Triumphant, she straightened and pumped her arm.

Which dislodged the broom, sending it sliding along the shelving unit. Above her, she heard a scraping noise, and when she looked up, the end of the broom had nudged something large that was bearing down on her.

Despite the uncannily prophetic sense of déjà vu, Carol didn't have time to put up her hand. Pain exploded in her head, then everything went…well, you know.

13

Someone was shaking Carol by the shoulder.

"Carol…wake up. We still have work to do. Carol?"

Carol resisted opening her eyes because part of her knew whatever "work" Gabrielle had for her would not be fun or pleasant.

"Carol!"

Her eyes popped open, sending a blinding pain through her temple. "*Ow, ow, ow.* What now?"

Standing above her, Gabrielle gave her a tight smile. "You don't have to be so testy, you know. This is your dream, not mine. It's not as if I'm getting paid."

Carol frowned. "It's because of your suggestion to seduce a man that I'm in this dilemma to begin with."

"That was an optional assignment. Let's get you up."

Gabrielle helped her to a sitting position. Carol grimaced. "The pain is worse this time."

Gabrielle made a rueful noise. "A person can take only so many hits."

"Do you think it's a sign that things are about to get worse?"

"Or better."

"Or worse," Carol pressed.

"Or worse," Gabrielle agreed.

"Has this happened to any of the other women in the book club?"

"Not to my knowledge," Gabrielle said.

Carol gestured to the monitor lying in the floor on its side. "Let's get this over with. What is it?"

"A look at Valentine's Day To Come."

Panic flowered in Carol's chest. "How far into the future?"

"Let's see."

Carol held up her hand. "I don't want to."

Gabrielle sat down on the floor next to Carol. "I know. And maybe that's why I'm here."

"What if I see something horrible...like what if I'm not even there?"

"Is that what you're afraid of?" Gabrielle asked. "That you'll die alone?"

Carol tried to think around the pain hammering her head. "Or maybe that I'll die *because* I'm alone."

Gabrielle laughed. "That's not true. When a woman gets married, her life expectancy actually goes down. Besides, you don't have to have a spouse or a lover to have a life rich with family and friends."

"I don't have family."

"I know. I'm sorry. But you could have your own someday."

"And..." Carol swallowed hard. "I don't have friends."

Gabrielle made a disbelieving noise. "Of course you have friends."

"No, I don't. I haven't kept up with childhood friends, and my coworkers hate me."

"That can't be true."

"It is. They call me names behind my back, like Ice Princess."

"You have the women in the book club."

"They don't like me either," Carol said.

"Of course they do."

"It's why I agreed to the seduction experiment," Carol admitted. "So they would like me. So I would fit in."

"I see." Gabrielle steepled her hands. "Why do you think you have trouble making friends?"

Carol shook her head. "I honestly don't know."

"Then why don't we take a look at the monitor and go from there?"

Carol chewed on a thumbnail while the monitor blinked on. The scene that materialized was a group of five women, perhaps in their eighties, sitting around a table, drinking coffee out of mugs with hearts on them. Carol scanned the faces, looking for herself. "I don't think any of those women are me."

Gabrielle turned up the volume.

"Those were the days," one woman was saying, "when books were actually made out of paper, when you could hold them in your hands and turn pages. Remember?"

The other women nodded, looking wistful.

"Cassie, how do you like your e-book reader?"

Gabrielle and Carol looked at each other. "That's our Cassie!"

"I love it," Cassie said, and when she smiled, Carol recognized the woman's bright blue eyes. "I can carry hundreds of books around with no problem. How about you, Page?"

Gabrielle and Carol laughed when they realized they were looking at the Red Tote Book Club circa fifty years into the future.

"I love it, too," Page said. "What I like best is that I can read the Red Tote Book Club selections on my e-reader and no one makes comments about an old lady reading dirty books!" Page Sharpe's auburn hair had faded, but she was still very pretty—in fact, all of the women had aged well.

As the conversation proceeded, they were able to identify the other women by their voices.

"Oh, my goodness, that's me!" Gabrielle said, pointing. "I'm completely white-headed!"

"But still beautiful," Carol said.

Gabrielle beamed.

Over the course of the next few minutes, they gathered that, amazingly, all the men the women had seduced as part of their book club assignment had become either a husband or significant other—and that all the couples seemed to still enjoy a frisky sex life.

But it became clear that Carol wasn't among the group, and the longer the scene played, the lower her heart hung.

"When was the last time anyone saw Carol Snow?" one of the women asked.

Carol sat forward.

They all made mournful noises and took the opportunity to sip their coffee. "I call her every few months and leave messages," Jacqueline Mays said. "But she never returns my calls."

"Me, too," said Wendy Trainer, still wearing her trademark pixie cut. "I never hear back from her."

"I send her a holiday card every year," Cassie said. "But I never get one in return."

Carol bit into her lip.

"I drove by her place once," the Gabrielle on the screen said. "I knocked on the door, but she didn't answer. Her neighbor said she hardly ever sees her. Says all she does is stay in and watch TV."

"Imagine that," Cassie said. "She still has a television."

"Didn't TVs go out of vogue about the same time as paper books?" Wendy asked.

"Sounds right," Jacqueline said. "God, we're old."

"But at least we have each other," Page said.

"That's right," they all chimed in, clinking their coffee cups.

"I just wish we could reconnect with Carol," Wendy said.

"If you remember," Cassie said, "she was always standoffish."

"Hard to get to know," Page agreed.

"And she didn't really participate that much," Jacqueline said.

"Maybe she likes being alone," Wendy added with a shrug.

In the end, all the women decided that yes, Carol must like being alone. Only the Gabrielle on the monitor said nothing, instead just sipped her coffee as the scene faded to black.

Carol blinked back desperate tears. "See? I'm destined to be alone."

Gabrielle clasped her hand. "You're not destined to be alone. You can control your personal relationships. So, after watching that future scene, why do you think you have trouble making friends?"

Carol sniffed and tried to collect herself. "Because I don't extend myself. Because I don't reach out to people and let them know I care. Because I don't lean on other people for support when I need it."

"All good reasons," Gabrielle said. "And you understand that you're going to have to change those behaviors to attract friends, and maybe lovers?"

She nodded. "Yes. And I will, if I ever get out of this endless loop I'm in."

Gabrielle pushed to her feet. "There's an old

truism that says, 'If you keep doing what you're doing, you'll keep getting what you've got.' To break out of your endless loop, maybe you need to do something unexpected."

Carol gingerly stood. "Like what?"

Gabrielle smiled. "That's up to you. It's time to say goodbye."

"I won't see you again?"

The woman smiled wide. "Every week at the Red Tote Book Club as long as you choose to. Good luck with your journey back."

Carol nodded and brushed her hands down the skirt of her Friday suit. Then she walked to the door of the storage room and let herself out in the hallway.

Her feet were heavy as she moved toward the elevator and her hands shook uncontrollably. She didn't want to be the old woman everyone in the scene on the monitor talked about—the recluse whose only pastime was watching TV. The woman who was alone.

Completely, absolutely, utterly alone.

As Carol approached the elevator, she noticed that once again, preparations were underway for the afternoon party. Red decorations of cupids and hearts abounded. Blowups of some of the company's Valentine's Day cards leaned against the wall, including the "take no prisoners" card she'd seen on her assistant's desk.

The volunteers shot unwelcome looks her way as she walked by.

If you keep doing what you're doing, you'll keep getting what you've got.

Carol pivoted and turned back. "Hi," she said to the group of about twenty. "My name is Carol and I work in the finance department. And I was wondering if you could tell me what you'd do with a thousand dollars if it fell out of the sky."

At first the employees were shy about speaking up, but the more probing questions that Carol asked about their families, eventually everyone opened up. She'd expected them to give answers such as a family vacation or a plasma television, not things like medical bills, car repairs, or a new heating unit for their home.

She enjoyed the conversation and appreciated their honesty. When she walked away, she had a better understanding of what kinds of daily financial obligations the average family faced—from school expenses to insurance to caring for elderly parents.

On the ride up to her floor, Carol turned to each person in the elevator and asked them a question about their job. At first, people looked at her warily. That's when Carol realized that people really did see her as cold and uncaring.

And why not? She hadn't given anyone a reason to think anything else—not potential friends and not potential lovers.

Luke's face floated into her mind. That was about to change she just hoped she wasn't too late.

14

When the elevator doors opened and Carol walked into her department, Tracy looked up from her desk where she was playing with her "new" computer. All around the bullpen, employees were comparing their machines and the peripheral equipment she and Luke had scavenged from the storage room the night before.

"Look at all this loot!" Tracy exclaimed. "I assume you had something to do with this. I know you've been trying to get the departmental budget increased for a couple of years now."

"I have," Carol said. "But I can't take credit for any of this. Luke Chancellor pulled strings and had unused machines from sales transferred over to our department. We owe him a huge debt of thanks."

Tracy blinked. "I thought you hated Luke Chancellor."

Carol pulsed with shame—what a bitter person she'd become over the years. James wasn't to blame—she'd allowed herself to get that way. "I'm sorry if I've given you or anyone else that impression. Of everything I know about Luke Chancellor, he's a decent and good man, and he's brought a lot of prosperity to our company."

Tracy angled her head. "Ms. Snow, are you okay?"

Carol gave a little laugh. "I'm a little tired and headachey, but overall, yeah, I'm good."

Tracy winced. "Uh…that would be my fault."

"What do you mean?"

Her assistant pointed to the coffeemaker in the corner. "I accidentally bought decaf coffee. So for the last week—no caffeine…which is probably why you've been tired and getting headaches." She gestured to the bullpen. "In fact, I think it's why everyone around here has been so cranky lately. I'm sorry if anyone has been rude." She cleared her throat. "Including me." She handed Carol a full steaming cup of coffee. "This should give you a boost and get rid of your headache."

Carol reached up to touch her forehead. "Thanks, but there's another reason—" She stopped when she couldn't find the lump that had been there before...many times. "Never mind," she murmured, perplexed anew.

"You're late for the directors' meeting," Tracy said. "Oh, and I revised the memo. You'll have a clean copy on your desk when you get back."

"Great—and thanks for the coffee."

Carol hurried to the room where the directors' meeting was held, but still took time to speak to coworkers along the way. Each time puzzled looks turned to genuine smiles, her mood buoyed higher.

Being the good guy felt...pretty darn good.

When she walked into the room, her fellow directors looked up and even though she sensed not all of them were happy to see her, she offered an apologetic smile to the room, then settled into an empty chair.

Her gaze swung to Luke, who sat at the head of the table. The sight of his handsome face took the breath from her lungs...she was head over heels in love with him. But she had to keep herself in check because as far as he was concerned, the only physical contact they'd had was a near-miss kiss in the storage room.

Luke offered her a friendly smile. "We were just getting ready to send out a search party for you, Carol."

"Sorry I'm late. I hope I didn't hold up the meeting."

"We heard a Good Samaritan delivered new computer equipment to your department this morning," Janet, the art director, said with a smile.

All gazes slid toward Luke. He held up his hands. "It was Carol's idea—I just... facilitated."

"Not true," Carol said. "It was Luke's idea, and he took care of everything. Everyone in my department is very happy, so I'd like to thank Luke publicly."

He seemed surprised by her speech, but pleased. "Okay, moving right along…we were about to take another vote on the issue of bonuses." He looked back to her. "I think it's pretty clear that anyone dissenting is following your lead, Carol, so I guess we can cut to the chase by asking if you've changed your mind about paying out a one-time employee bonus of one thousand dollars?"

The weight of a roomful of stares shifted to her. Luke looked hopeful, and Carol knew he was thinking of her comment in the storage room last night that she might reconsider her position.

So many things had happened since last night…where to start?

Carol took a deep breath. "As a matter of fact…yes, I have changed my mind. I've had a chance to talk to a small sample of employees and I realize now what a one-time payment of a thousand dollars can do for a family and for employee morale. If we can't afford to reward everyone when we've had a good year, then when can we? I recommend that we approve bonuses immediately."

Luke's eyes widened in surprise, then a smile broke over his face. "All in favor?" It was a unanimous vote. Luke could barely contain his enthusiasm—it endeared him to her that much more. He gave her a little nod of thanks that made her heart squeeze…and scared her a little. How could she feel so close to him in such a short period of time? And would his feelings ever "catch up" with hers?

Carol left the meeting and when she reached her department, everyone was in a celebratory mood—apparently word of the approval of the bonuses had leaked out and maybe the coffee change had helped, too. Her own headache had vanished and her energy level had returned. Carol circulated with her employees as they inspected their new computers. When she made it into her office, she decided to leave the door open to draw on the infectious creative energy of the group.

Carol had another reason to be happy—the red skies were gone. Meaning, there would be no blizzard…which didn't matter anyway because she was eager to go to the company party this time and have fun.

And see Luke.

She had a hard time concentrating on the mountain of paperwork on her desk, even though she had it memorized by now. She was antsy waiting for Luke to knock on her door and ask her to walk down with him to the party. If they got together at the party, he would ask her to Valentine's Day dinner tomorrow night—like all the times before—instead of the blonde she'd seen in her vision. And this time, she'd say yes. Carol kept checking her lipstick in the tiny mirror in her desk drawer, reminding herself she needed to play it a little cool.

While she had a free minute, though, she pulled out her phone and sent Gabrielle a happy update via text message.

Forget seduction—I've surrendered to love.

A couple of minutes later, Gabrielle replied.

Glad you found a way to break the continuous loop.

Carol squinted. "What the?" It was almost as if the real Gabrielle had been privy to...

No, that couldn't be.

A knock sounded at her door.

Her heart surged when she saw Luke standing there, looking gorgeous in his brown slacks and pale blue dress shirt, minus a tie. "Come in."

"Hey, I like your new open-door policy. Wish more directors thought like us."

She warmed under his praise and reminded herself she wasn't supposed to know why he'd dropped by. "To what do I owe this pleasure?"

He crossed to her desk and picked up a ball of rubber bands. "I just wanted to stop by and thank you for reconsidering your position on the employee bonuses. You made a lot of people happy today."

"The credit is yours, Luke. Not only was it your idea, but it's under your leadership that sales has thrived." She gave him a warm smile. "We're lucky to have you."

He stared at her, but his eyes were unreadable. "Thank you."

Suddenly he replaced the ball on her desk and stepped back. "I'd better get going."

"Wait," she said, reaching for her briefcase and coat. "I'll walk down to the party with you."

"Uh, actually...I'm not going to the party."

Disappointment zigzagged through her. "But...the party was your idea."

He nodded. "I know."

She desperately cast around for more excuses to get him to the party. "And...the bonus checks will be given out. I thought you'd want to be there for that."

"I do, but...something came up. I was invited to a Steeplechase and since the weather is so nice this afternoon I decided to go."

Carol swallowed hard. "Steeplechase, huh?"

She had a clear memory of a leggy, busty blonde smiling up at him. *I guess it was my lucky day when I decided to go with my friend to the Steeplechase...I never dreamed I'd meet someone like you, Luke.*

And just like that, Carol remembered the icicle card that Luke had planted in her book club tote bag. That was what he truly thought of her…the Ice Princess who wouldn't thaw. All of this flirtation…all of this buttering up was really to get her support for his bonus program. And now that he had what he wanted, he was pulling back. She could sense it…could see it in his eyes…in the way he avoided her.

"Uh, yeah," he said, then shrugged awkwardly. "You know—horses jumping and… stuff. Sounds…interesting." He couldn't seem to make eye contact.

Carol smiled and nodded, not trusting herself to speak. How ironic that she'd finally opened her heart to a man—and to others because of him—and he didn't want her.

She was two for two. First James, now Luke.

But underneath the hurt and disappointment, there was gratitude. Because without Luke's merciless teasing and prodding, she never would've tried to enact revenge on him…and never would've come to realize how she'd been sporting a Back Off sign on her forehead. That by closing herself off to the hurtful things in life, like loss and rejection, she'd also closed herself off to the good things in life, like love and sensuality.

And even friendship.

So…tomorrow night while Luke was taking Blondie out on the town, Carol would be on the phone, going down a list of old friends that she'd lost touch with and trying to reconnect.

With jerky body language, Luke pointed to the door. "So…we could share an elevator down."

"Sounds good," she said, with the nicest smile she could manage considering her heart was breaking. She'd have to get used to working with him and hiding her feelings. She draped her coat over her arm and picked up her briefcase. They walked to the elevator. Her mind raced to concoct small talk, but she couldn't seem to come up with anything.

Luke pushed the call button, then whistled under his breath, obviously wanting to be anywhere else. Carol felt foolish for suggesting they ride down together. When the car finally came, they walked on, instantly going to opposite sides. He pushed Lobby and she pushed

Basement. The doors closed and they started their downward descent.

"So…" Luke alternated looking at the ceiling and at his feet. "I guess the rumor is true."

Carol lifted her eyebrows. "What rumor?"

Luke shrugged. "The reason you're in such a good mood all of a sudden."

She froze. "What reason would that be?"

"Because of a man."

Carol wanted to die on the spot. The only thing worse than pining for a man is him *knowing* you're pining for him. Her mind sprinted ahead—what would the women in the book club advise her to do?

And the answer came to her instantly: *Lie.*

"There *is* a man," Carol admitted, but she was unable to look at Luke—she was afraid he'd see in her eyes that it was him she was crazy about.

"Oh," he nodded. "That's good. Anyone I would know?"

"No," she said emphatically. "You and he would never cross paths." Not a lie, actually.

The doors dinged open to the lobby and not a second too soon. Luke stepped off then turned around. "I'm glad you found someone, Snow. Hope you and your boyfriend have a nice Valentine's dinner."

"Thank you," she said. "Enjoy Richardson's."

As the doors closed, he was squinting and mouthing, "Richardson's?"

15

After her humiliating exchange with Luke about the rumor that a man accounted for her new good mood, Carol was tempted to skip the company party and go home to watch TV shows on her DVR. The only thing that stopped her was the memory of the Red Tote Book Club members as seniors describing her as a recluse. In time the rumor mill would die down. In the meantime, she meant to adhere to her new philosophy of extending herself to coworkers.

She could hear the noise of the party even before the elevator stopped. When the doors opened, the full force of music, laughter and voices blasted her. Her stomach churned, both at the known and the unknown, but with an underlying excitement about the new outlook she had on people and relationships in general. A few heads turned in her direction and Carol extended a smile. When they reciprocated, she moved forward to properly introduce herself.

The party was fun, and a great place to practice her newfound skills. When she spotted her assistant Tracy, she walked over to say hello.

"I didn't get to tell you before you left," Carol said with a smile, "but the memo is top-notch."

Tracy dimpled. "Really?"

"Really. Perfect grammar, spelling, and just a well-written piece of documentation."

"Thank you, Ms. Snow."

Carol touched the young woman's hand. "No, thank you, Tracy, for all the things you do for me and for helping to keep the department running."

Tracy stared at her, then burst into tears.

Carol blinked and patted her shoulder. "What on earth? What's wrong, Tracy?"

"I did something really mean."

Carol shook her head. "I can't imagine you would do something that mean."

Tracy nodded her head like a little girl. "I did it, and I'm sorry."

"What did you do?"

The young woman pressed her lips together, then blurted, "I put a card comparing you to an icicle in one of your bags."

Carol's eyebrows went up. "That was you?"

"I'm so sorry, Ms. Snow. It was a very mean, immature thing to do. I wouldn't blame you if you fired me."

Carol thought back to all the times she'd had nothing but criticism and harsh words for her assistant, and squeezed the redhead's shoulders. "I wouldn't dream of firing you. But thank you for telling me."

Tracy excused herself to repair her makeup, which left Carol alone with a new revelation.

So Luke Chancellor hadn't planted the unflattering card in her tote bag after all. She shook her head. And yet she'd been determined to make that man suffer for something he hadn't even done.

And yes, she was glad to know that he hadn't thought so poorly of her.

She looked in the direction of the storage room, half afraid to go near it, but conceding that one loose end begged to be tied up: her lost earring.

Carol's heart began to thump and she found her feet moving toward the room that still represented so many secrets and mysticisms that she wasn't sure she should go back inside. On the other hand, what kind of nut believed in a time travel portal in the storage room of a greeting card company?

Carol pursed her mouth.

A company named "Mystic Touch."

The hallway leading to the storage room was dark and quiet. The closer she got to the door, the more she felt drawn to the room—compelled to go inside. She punched in the access code and waited for the click, then pushed open the door, walked inside, and flipped on all the lights. Her pulse pounded, on alert for any falling equipment that might take her back to the beginning of this day. Today had been the best version so far, and she wouldn't want to try to top it. Even if Luke had decided not to come to the party.

The door to the storage room clicked, then opened…and Luke stepped inside.

Carol felt her jaw loosen and wondered for a split second if her mind was playing tricks on her again.

"I thought I might find you here," he said.

"I came in to look for an earring I lost last night," she murmured.

"Last night seems…like a long time ago," Luke ventured.

Carol could only nod. "You changed your mind about the party?"

He walked toward her. "Yes. I came back to make a fool out of myself."

Her heart tripped harder against her breastbone. "What do you mean?"

"I know you've met someone," he said, stepping closer. "But…why not me?"

Carol's heart soared. She covered her mouth and tears began to stream down her cheeks.

Luke stood in front of her with an anguished expression on his face as he retrieved a handkerchief from his back pocket. "You have to interpret tears for me. Happy? Sad? Toothache?"

"Happy," she said, laughing and dabbing at her tears. "The man I met, the one who's put me in such a good mood?"

"Yeah," he said warily.

"It's you."

"Me?" His eyebrows drew together and he got a faraway look in his eyes, as if he was trying hard to remember something elusive. "Me," he said, nodding, then pulled his hand over his mouth. "Look, if I've seemed different lately, it's because after that night here in the storage room where I almost kissed you, I started having these very...*vivid* fantasies and...*feelings*..."

Carol stepped close to him and lifted her arms to loop around his neck. "I think I know what you mean."

Luke kissed her, moaning into her mouth until the vibration echoed through her body. He pulled her against him and their hands became frenzied, roaming over each other's bodies. He smoothed his palms down her back, over her buttocks, and pulled her sex against the hardened ridge of his erection. The physical proof of what they were going to do…again…and again…and again…made her dizzy with lust.

"Let's find your earring," he whispered, "so we can get out of here."

"Never mind," she said, urging him toward the door.

"It must be important to you. Let's do at least one quick pass. If we don't see it, we'll take off."

Since he was determined, she relented. "I have the other earring so you'll know what it looks like."

When she pulled the mismatched one from her briefcase, Luke frowned slightly at her briefcase, as if it seemed familiar to him, then took the earring. As Carol followed Luke up and down the aisles, her nerves jangled. She just wanted to leave. Things were good the way they were…things were perfect, in fact. Why mess with it?

"Is that it?" Luke asked, pointing to the base of a shelving unit. "I think it is." He crouched, down, but Carol couldn't watch. She held her breath, waiting for a crashing noise.

"Carol?"

She opened her eyes to see him dangling the earring in front of her. "Are you okay?" he asked.

She nodded. "Thank you."

"You're welcome, although it bodes well for me, too," he offered. "Emeralds are the symbol of a successful love."

Carol stared up at him, incredulous. "I'd heard that." She palmed the earring. "Let's go. Hurry. Before something...happens."

But at the door, one thing made her turn back. "Aren't you forgetting something?"

Luke frowned. "What?"

"The candy you bought me?"

He squinted at her. "How do you know about the candy?"

"I just do," she said, crossing her arms.

"It's not much," he said, reaching high on a shelf to remove a heart-shaped box of chocolates. When he handed her the box, his cheeks were tinged pink. The red silk box read "I Love You."

Surprise sparkled in her chest at the romantic gesture.

Luke scratched his head. "To be honest,

I'm not quite sure why I bought that one. It just seemed…right. I feel like…I know you, Carol…more than I do…"

Apparently deciding actions spoke louder than words, he lowered his mouth toward hers. She lifted her mouth to accept his kiss, sighing through the overlapping of sensations that were both new and familiar. Far removed from their first kiss, her mind and body still reeled from the raw power in Luke's probing tongue.

He lifted his head and looked into her eyes. "Do you believe in déjà vu?"

"Oh, yes," she whispered, then curled her hand around his neck and pulled his lips down on hers, hard.

*Who could have guessed that a few
sexy books could make such a difference
in a woman's life? But not all books are as
serious as the ones Carol and her friends
have been studying. In fact, some can be
even quite magical!*

*For those of you looking to add a little
fantasy to your sensual reading, check out:*

*Blazing Bedtime Stories, Volume IV
by Kimberly Raye and Samantha Hunter.
Available next month.*

Here's a sneak peek.

1

This was the *last* place he needed to be.

The warning echoed in Rayne Montana's head as he stood in the shadows outside the Iron Horseshoe—a small bar and grill that sat on the outskirts of Skull Creek, Texas. He was only in town for a week. The fewer locals he ran into, the better.

Hell, the fewer *people* he came into contact with, the better.

At the same time, the Horseshoe was the only decent bar in his map dot of a hometown, and pretty much the only place on a Tuesday night that a man could find a woman.

And Rayne needed a woman in the worst possible way.

He pushed through the door, into the neon-lit interior. Anticipation hit him like a sucker punch to the gut. Hotter and more potent than anything he'd ever felt before, and he'd always been a lusty man.

It was different now.

He was different.

His body vibrated. His muscles clenched. His senses magnified, his perception heightened to a new level that had nothing to do with fourteen years of special ops training as part of an elite Navy SEAL unit, and everything to do with the hunger that now lived and breathed inside of him.

He was clear across the room, yet his nostrils flared with the rich lilac scent of a woman sitting near the jukebox. His razor sharp vision sliced through the cigarette haze to see a tiny spider web near the far corner of the tin ceiling. Taylor Swift blared from the juke box, but the song didn't drown out the subtle slide of boots against the sawdust floor.

He heard *everything*—the *glub-glub* as a man chugged a beer near the pool table, the sizzle of burgers popping on the grill out back, the hum of the Coors sign that flickered on the wall, the sharp intake of breath when the woman behind the bar turned and spotted him.

He stiffened and awareness skittered up his spine. He turned and found the bluest eyes in the Texas Hill Country staring back at him.

Need knifed through him. Fierce. Overwhelming. Unexpected.

Because she wasn't just one of the dozens of women he'd had in the past few weeks as he'd tried to sate the craving deep in his gut.

She was the one woman he'd wanted all of his life.

The one woman who hadn't wanted him.

She turned and took off for the back room, obviously desperate to avoid him. His chest tightened and pain twisted inside of him. A crazy reaction, he knew. So what if Lucy Rivers still hated his guts?

He wasn't here for her.

She'd been his girl way back in the day and he'd been her man, but that had ended a long, *long* time ago. He hadn't seen her in the four-

teen years since. Hell, he didn't *want* to see
her.

Especially now.

He ignored the small voice that whispered
otherwise and forced his attention back to the
sharp need pushing and pulling inside of him.
Walking the few feet to an empty table, he
pulled out a chair and sank down, his back to
the wall.

He scoped out the room, his gaze going to a
blonde that sat nearby. The minute his attention
zeroed in on her, she felt him. She turned. Her
brown eyes collided with his. Interest sparked
in her gaze and her thoughts rolled through his
head as clearly as if they'd been his own.

Her name was Sherry and she was a local
real estate agent. She'd just sold her first house
this afternoon and she was here celebrating.
She'd left the husband and the kids at home
and she was now on her fourth margarita. She'd
never had an affair before, but the minute her
gaze locked with Rayne's she was suddenly
more than willing.

She would gladly peel off her clothes. Spread
her legs. Do any and everything he wanted—

He broke the connection and shifted his attention elsewhere. As starved as he was, he wasn't about to add *bastard home wrecker* to his ever-growing list of sins. His gaze went to the next woman.

She had red hair. Green eyes. Nice smile. Her name was different, but her reaction was the same. She wanted him.

They all did.

He shifted his attention from one female to the next. Some smiled. Some licked their lips. Others waved. One even leaned over just so, giving him a spectacular view of her bare breasts topped with rosy red nipples.

There was no doubt. They wanted sex.

And he wanted it, too.

As fiercely as he wanted the succulent heat of their blood in his mouth, gliding down his throat, filling his body.

A *vampire*.

He still had trouble wrapping his mind around the concept, but there was no other explanation for what had happened to him that night two weeks ago in the Afghan mountains outside of Kabul.

For what *was* happening to him.

Right here. Right now.

His body ached. His insides knotted and twisted. Electricity skimmed up and down his arms, making him feel more alive than ever before. Ironic considering he was stone cold dead.

He had been. For those few brief moments before he'd swallowed the blood of his attacker, he'd been limp. Lifeless.

No more. A few ravenous sips and he'd turned into something dark. Dangerous.

A vampire who fed off of blood *and* sex.

But not tonight.

Tonight was about drinking in the sweet, decadent energy of a woman's climax. He'd figured out early on that if he did that, he could escape the bloodlust a little longer and keep his fangs to himself.

Hopefully.

His attention shifted to the doorway where Lucy had disappeared. The urge to go after her hit him hard and fast despite the fact that he'd learned his lesson long ago where she was concerned. He'd trusted her and she'd broken his heart.

She'd dumped him without a word of explanation. Just a quick "It's over" that had cut like a dull blade straight into his heart. And damned if he'd ever understood why.

Sure, he'd wanted to ask.

To plead and beg even.

But where some kids had been raised with nice clothes and good food and a loving family, Rayne had grown up the son of an alcoholic father and a neglectful mother. He'd had nothing but his pride. And so he'd kept his distance until he'd left for West Point.

He hadn't looked back since.

But things had changed in the past few weeks.

He'd changed, and the only person likely to do any begging should they come face-to-face was little Miss Lucy.

For his kiss.

His touch.

His cock.

His body stirred and he grew harder. Hungrier. In spite of it all, she *had* given him some of the best sex of his life. She'd been as wild as he'd been, and just as uninhibited. Together they'd been explosive.

A perfect match.

Or so he'd thought.

Memories stirred and images rolled through his head. He saw Lucy's smiling face. Felt her small hand in his. Heard the sweet sound of her laughter.

His chest tightened and bitterness welled inside of him, along with something else. A deep-seated curiosity. She might have faked being happy with him, but had she faked the chemistry, too?

Maybe.

Probably.

Get over it, buddy.

Solid advice, he knew. But while she'd made it more than clear at the end that she felt zilch for him emotionally, he couldn't help but wonder if she would still react to him physically.

If she would squirm when he bit her nipple and dig her nails into his shoulders when he licked her clit and gasp when he plunged hilt deep inside of her.

There was only one way to find out.

He pushed to his feet and went after her.

He was *here*.

The truth snapped at Lucy's heels and followed her through the rear EXIT and out into the gravel parking lot behind the bar. Panic punched her in the chest as she leaned back against the building. Her palms flattened against the cool tin and she tried to calm her pounding heart.

What the hell was wrong with her?

She was Lucy *Rivers*. She didn't run from men. Hell, she *liked* men. Maybe not as often as some might think, but enough to feed the bad girl reputation she'd inherited from her late mother and older sister.

Then again, this wasn't just any man.

This was *the* man. The one who'd made her tummy quiver and her knees quake.

Fourteen years ago, she reminded herself. No way should he have the same effect now.

Her traitorous hands trembled and she stiffened.

Okay, so her body was definitely in overdrive,

but not because she was still hooked on him. It was simply the shock of seeing him out of the blue that had her heart pounding so fiercely.

He'd been so busy all these years with the military—first West Point, then special ops training, then mission after mission. He'd been too busy to come home to Texas. Not that he would have wanted to. His father had been a bastard and his mother hadn't been much better. It was no wonder Rayne hadn't bothered to show up when the old man had passed away three years ago from a heart attack.

Shortly after that, Rayne's mother had abandoned the run-down farm, packed up and moved to Arizona with some guy she'd picked up at a truck stop. With his only family gone, he'd had no ties to Skull Creek and so Lucy had given up on ever having to face him.

Shock.

That's what had her pulse racing and her hands shaking and her nipples throbbing.

"That, or maybe you're just glad to see me."

His deep, sultry voice came from out of nowhere, whispering through her head, sending her hormones into a tizzy. Lucy knew then that she could no longer avoid a confrontation. The time had come.

Rayne Montana was finally here.

And he was standing right behind her.

*Rancher Ramsey Westmoreland's
temporary cook
is way too attractive for his liking.
Little does he know Chloe Burton
came to his ranch
with another agenda entirely...*

That man across the street had to be, without a doubt, the most handsome man she'd ever seen.

Chloe Burton's pulse beat rhythmically as he stopped to talk to another man in front of a feed store. He was tall, dark and every inch of sexy—from his Stetson to the well-worn leather boots on his feet. And from the way his jeans and Western shirt fit his broad muscular shoulders, it was quite obvious he had everything it took to separate the men from the boys. The combination was enough to corrupt any woman's mind and had her weakening even from a distance. Her body felt flushed. It was hot. Unsettled.

Over the past year the only male who had gotten her time and attention had been the e-mail. That was simply pathetic, especially since now she was practically drooling simply at the sight of a man. Even his stance—both hands in his jeans pockets, legs braced apart, was a pose she would carry to her dreams.

And he was smiling, evidently enjoying the conversation being exchanged. He had dimples, incredibly sexy dimples in not one but both cheeks.

"What are you staring at, Clo?"

Chloe nearly jumped. She'd forgotten she had a lunch date. She glanced over the table at her best friend from college, Lucia Conyers.

"Take a look at that man across the street in the blue shirt, Lucia. Will he not be perfect for Denver's first issue of *Simply Irresistible* or what?" Chloe asked with so much excitement she almost couldn't stand it.

She was the owner of *Simply Irresistible,* a magazine for today's up-and-coming woman.

Their once-a-year Irresistible Man cover, which highlighted a man the magazine felt deserved the honor, had increased sales enough for Chloe to open a Denver office.

When Lucia didn't say anything but kept staring, Chloe's smile widened. "Well?"

Lucia glanced across the booth at her. "Since you asked, I'll tell you what I see. One of the Westmorelands—Ramsey Westmoreland. And yes, he'd be perfect for the cover, but he won't do it."

Chloe raised a brow. "He'd get paid for his services, of course."

Lucia laughed and shook her head. "Getting paid won't be the issue, Clo—Ramsey is one of the wealthiest sheep ranchers in this part of Colorado. But everyone knows what a private person he is. Trust me—he won't do it."

Chloe couldn't help but smile. The man was the epitome of what she was looking for in a magazine cover and she was determined that whatever it took, he would be it.

"Umm, I don't like that look on your face, Chloe. I've seen it before and know exactly what it means."

She watched as Ramsey Westmoreland entered the store with a swagger that made her almost breathless. She *would* be seeing him again.

Look for Silhouette Desire's
HOT WESTMORELAND NIGHTS
by
Brenda Jackson,
available March 9
wherever books are sold.

SPECIAL EDITION

FROM *USA TODAY* BESTSELLING AUTHOR
CHRISTINE RIMMER

A BRIDE FOR JERICHO BRAVO

Marnie Jones had long ago buried her wild-child
impulses and opted to be "safe," romantically
speaking. But one look at born rebel Jericho Bravo
and she began to wonder if her thrill-seeking side
was about to be revived. Because if ever there was
a man worth taking a chance on, there he was,
right within her grasp....

*Available in March
wherever books are sold.*

REQUEST YOUR FREE BOOKS!

2 FREE NOVELS
PLUS 2
FREE GIFTS!

HARLEQUIN®

Blaze

Red-hot reads!

YES! Please send me 2 FREE Harlequin® Blaze™ novels and my 2 FREE gifts (gifts are worth about $10). After receiving them, if I don't wish to receive any more books, I can return the shipping statement marked "cancel." If I don't cancel, I will receive 6 brand-new novels every month and be billed just $4.24 per book in the U.S. or $4.71 per book in Canada. That's a saving of close to 15% off the cover price. It's quite a bargain. Shipping and handling is just 50¢ per book in the U.S. and 75¢ per book in Canada.* I understand that accepting the 2 free books and gifts places me under no obligation to buy anything. I can always return a shipment and cancel at any time. Even if I never buy another book, the two free books and gifts are mine to keep forever.

151 HDN E4CY   351 HDN E4CN

Name _____ (PLEASE PRINT) _____

Address _____ Apt. #

City _____ State/Prov. _____ Zip/Postal Code

Signature (if under 18, a parent or guardian must sign)

Mail to the **Harlequin Reader Service:**
IN U.S.A.: P.O. Box 1867, Buffalo, NY 14240-1867
IN CANADA: P.O. Box 609, Fort Erie, Ontario L2A 5X3

Not valid for current subscribers to Harlequin Blaze books.

Want to try two free books from another line?
Call 1-800-873-8635 or visit www.morefreebooks.com.

* Terms and prices subject to change without notice. Prices do not include applicable taxes. N.Y. residents add applicable sales tax. Canadian residents will be charged applicable provincial taxes and GST. Offer not valid in Quebec. This offer is limited to one order per household. All orders subject to approval. Credit or debit balances in a customer's account(s) may be offset by any other outstanding balance owed by or to the customer. Please allow 4 to 6 weeks for delivery. Offer available while quantities last.

Your Privacy: Harlequin Books is committed to protecting your privacy. Our Privacy Policy is available online at www.eHarlequin.com or upon request from the Reader Service. From time to time we make our lists of customers available to reputable third parties who may have a product or service of interest to you. If you would prefer we not share your name and address, please check here. ☐

Help us get it right—We strive for accurate, respectful and relevant communications. To clarify or modify your communication preferences, visit us at www.ReaderService.com/consumerschoice.

HB10

COMING NEXT MONTH

Available February 23, 2010

www.eHarlequin.com